T0129069

BANTHOM

RODNEY WETZEL

ARCHWAY
PUBLISHING

Archway Publishing books may be ordered
through booksellers or by contacting:

Archway Publishing
1663 Liberty Drive
Bloomington, IN 47403
www.archwaypublishing.com
1 (888) 242-5904

Because of the dynamic nature of the Internet, any web
addresses or links contained in this book may have changed
since publication and may no longer be valid. The views
expressed in this work are solely those of the author and do
not necessarily reflect the views of the publisher, and the
publisher hereby disclaims any responsibility for them.

Any people depicted in stock imagery provided
by Thinkstock are models, and such images are
being used for illustrative purposes only.
Certain stock imagery © Thinkstock.

ISBN: 978-1-4808-5779-7 (sc)
ISBN: 978-1-4808-5780-3 (e)

Library of Congress Control Number: 2018900980

Print information available on the last page.

Archway Publishing rev. date: 09/24/2018

Dedicated to my beautiful sister, Jill
Marienfeld, whom I love so very much

PREFACE

A bby Lane looked up at the star-filled sky, and the reality of what was taking place hit her like a bolt of lightning. Though she felt like screaming, she could not. Though she felt like fighting, she could not. Everything was now in the hands of the demonic creature. As it dragged her cruelly along by the hair of her head, pain occupied her whole being. There was nothing she could do. From the instant she'd peered into those cavernous brown eyes, she'd been helpless—paralyzed. She could hear the *flop-flop-flop* of the creature's feet striking the road ahead, smell the intensity of its stench, feel the scraping of her bare arms and back on the payment, and taste the blood from her lips where she had hit the ground. Her senses were not only working; they were in overdrive, yet she could not move a muscle. The creature had mesmerized her and put her in a trance with its beautiful brown eyes.

Abby felt her head collide with the curb as the creature pulled her off the road and up onto the grass. *It's heading toward the bay,* she thought, trying to clear her foggy mind. She could smell the ocean air. She was certain of what would happen there. There would be no happy ending—no last chance to tell her baby girl goodbye. She knew the creature was going to kill her.

Above her, she saw car lights pirouetting across the night sky, and a burst of optimism hit her. She gave everything she could to make a sound, but regrettably, nothing came out. She felt the creature quicken its pace to a trot as the top of a tree came into view above her; it was hiding. Maybe someone had seen. Maybe there was still hope. Maybe she would be the damsel saved from the demon's clutches in the moment before her death, like in all those classic Hollywood movies. As quickly as they had appeared, the lights died out. She could distinguish the sound of a car as it passed close by. *So close,* she thought, yet they could not see that she was lying right there, plain as day. *What the hell is the matter with you fucking people?* she wondered.

She felt the creature's claws tighten their grip on her pain-ridden scalp as the demon gradually emerged from its sanctuary. There was no urgency in its steps—no eagerness to reach its destination—just a slow, methodical pace farther into the darkness. Her thoughts went to her daughter,

Lucy, who had just celebrated her fourth birthday. She was at home with her grandma. Abby could picture them getting the news, and she could sense the aching in their hearts. *God, please help me. My baby is so small. For her sake, please help me. Send this monster back to hell. I know you are a strong, loving God. Don't let this happen.*

The creature seemed to sense her thoughts, for it paused and glared down at her. Its face was that of a horrific corpse, only this cadaver's face was broken and twisted to the point one could not call it human. Its teeth shone in the darkness. They were oversize and jagged, like those of a feeding shark. They pressed together in a malevolent grin, as if the creature knew her prayers would go unanswered. It stared at her for a moment and then turned and ambled on.

The smell of the ocean was getting stronger, and the sound of the waves was more prevalent. What would it do when it got her to wherever it was going? How was it going to finish her? A million horrifying visions swept through her mind all at once. The fear was overwhelming. *Just do it, and get it over with, you bastard.* Then her mind used its last line of defense: she passed out.

CHAPTER 1

THE JOURNEY

Dublin, June 8, 1998

Sixty-five-year-old Dr. Timothy Hoffman, a native of New Jersey, shuffled his rounded five-foot-five body down Parnell Street, carrying his oversize umbrella. Though the morning was bright and sunny, the weather called for rain later in the day. He was heading for Patrick Conway's Pub. It was his second day off from University College Dublin, and he was going to enjoy every minute of it. His apartment was on the corner of Dominick Street Lower and Parnell Street. It wasn't the greatest fucking place he had ever lived, but it was close to damn near everything. The pub was said to be the oldest in Dublin, and he liked that. He liked things that were old instead of young and uppity like those bastard students of his. Teaching was a living but not his passion. God knew he was never going to make money off parapsychology, so he had to put up with all that bullshit to fulfill his true life's adventure.

During his summer, winter, and spring breaks, Hoffman investigated haunted locations. He had a vast knowledge of the latest types of ghost-hunting equipment, though he was not good at setting them up or maintaining them. He always made sure he had the best and brightest student geek for those tasks. He also made sure to hire the best student he could find to be his personal assistant. The right assistant would help in booking flights and rooms, making phone calls, conducting historical backgrounds, paying staff, and, most importantly, getting written permissions.

Hoffman recalled taking a trip with his uncle Robert down to St. Augustine, Florida, when he was a lad. Uncle Robert had traveled a lot for work and always had been hounding someone to venture with him to this state or that. He'd sold something. Hoffman could not remember for sure what it had been—maybe some kind of insurance or savings plan, he thought. It had been something along those lines. No one in the family had enjoyed going with him on those escapades, because Uncle Robert had been a chatterbox, and his old 1941 Nash Ambassador 600 had smelled of cigars and perspiration. Hoffman remembered it as constantly cluttered with old maps, sandwich bags, beer bottles, and other assorted junk. That never had seemed to bother Uncle Robert, who'd taken no notice of the mess, probably because he'd spent much of his life on the road. He'd always stayed at run-down motels, the kind that used to dot the highways before hotel chains, such as Holiday Inn and Best Western, had sprung up just about everywhere. That time had been no different.

After his uncle left for his appointments, the young Dr. Hoffman decided he was not going to spend the day in a musty old motel room with only a broken radio to keep him company. He took off on his own, even though he had promised his uncle he would not, to explore what his uncle claimed to be the oldest city in the United States. The first thing he passed was a time-worn cemetery filled with tattered white stones whose inscriptions were so faded that many were hard to read. Though only ten at the time, Hoffman had been to the graves of his grandparents, two uncles, and a great-aunt multiple times—every Memorial Day, in fact, to plant; every birthday to bring fresh flowers; and every Labor Day to leave pots of artificial flowers that could withstand the winter's bitter cold. Not once had he ever felt uncomfortable about being among the dead, but even at its edge, that cemetery seemed ominous, and he quickened his pace. As he strolled through the deep-rooted tabby gates of the city, he looked over at the old fort still standing after all those years. *Man, it looks like it was built yesterday*, he thought. He could not keep himself from imagining a great battle taking place, with pirate ships firing cannons upon the mighty fortress, which would cast volley after volley in response.

As he walked down St. George, he came to a run-down building and read the sign: Oldest School. *School? Perish the thought.* That was his vacation. On the side of the wooden structure sat a little girl reading a book. She was dressed in an attractive white dress with a matching white bonnet. She smiled at him as he sauntered by, and then she stood and waved her arms for him to follow. Hoffman, entranced by her attractiveness, did as she instructed. Around the back of the old schoolhouse was a back door they entered together. They walked through an insignificant breezeway into what appeared to be a classroom with level wooden benches. The little girl patted the seat next to her for the young Dr. Hoffman to perch, and he did so without question. There was something about the soft light radiating around her that brought comfort to him, a feeling of serenity. She returned to reading her book but looked up every few minutes and offered a heartening smile, which young Hoffman was more than willing to return.

A large woman dressed much like the little girl

in a bonnet, white dress, and apron came bouncing through the door. "Come, children, and see what school was like in the olden days," she said. As she turned to enter, she stopped when she saw him sitting there. "I am sorry, young man, but are you with this group?"

"No. I'm sorry. I just walked in with her," he said, pointing to his right.

"Who?" the woman asked.

Young Hoffman turned and looked at empty space. There was no little girl; she and her worn, ragged book were gone. "But she was right here a minute ago."

"Well, that's okay, but if you are not part of this group, I will have to ask you to leave, dear."

Hoffman stood in amazement and then started for the door. As he was walking past the woman, she bent over and quietly whispered, "That's okay, honey. I see her too sometimes."

From that day on, he'd been hooked. There was something past that life, and he was going to show it to the world. For many years, he had traveled across the planet from one country to the next, doing his investigations. He had seen a lot of unexplainable things occur, but he had never caught a life force on film. If only he could show the world what he had seen. If only he could prove the existence of life after death. The Banthom House might hold the proof he needed. Its long reputation of being the home of a known Satanist and reports of spirits sighted walking in front of its windows late at night had been enough to spark his interest, but after current events, it was even more alluring. From what he had read in the paper, someone had cut a boy's throat and hung him upside down, and a girl had been ripped apart at the midsection at the Banthom place. He knew their spirits might not be anything like the peaceful, shining specter he had once had a face-to-face with, but dammit, something was going on there. Surely after an event like that, one would expect unsettled spirits. Still, if he could only get a glimpse on film, it would be worth it. Thank God for Josette and the two Americans. They were the key to getting into the house. Josette's reputation for helping solve hard cases for Scotland Yard was well known in certain circles. Even though he himself was skeptical of mediums, she had earned her right to investigate the house, and the current owner would never have thought of saying no.

In the morning, he was meeting with the two professors from the States. With any luck, they would have deep pockets, and if he was truly lucky, they might fund the entire investigation. He didn't give a rat's ass about them or what they wanted from the deal, but he needed them for cash and access to the house. Hoffman knew all too well the owner would be astonished that he had them on board.

He began to cross Parnell Square West, when a horn blasted for him to get out of the way. "Asshole!" he huffed in response, and he kept his course. At the pub, he was meeting an old student, one who had been part of the response team the night the two youngsters were killed. Since the news had broken, he had dedicated his time to studying everything there was to know about the murders. He knew that after a few pints, the kid would spill his guts, and he would have the final piece of the puzzle.

If there was one certainty in life for Phillip Parker, it was that he hated Detroit Metro. The airport seemed to have been put together on a whim with no rhyme or reason. It consisted of endless walkways of disgruntled travelers and endless terminals. The Holiday Inn where they had stayed the night before was nice enough, and best of all, it was clean. He was thankful for a good night's sleep—his first since planning the venture.

Thank God Franky is so obsessive with everything he does, he thought as he fumbled through his pocket to make sure the tickets were still in place. Franky had set up and double-checked everything: the rental car, the tickets, lodging, the package to Mrs.

Cartwright, and, most importantly, the directions for the entire trip. Phillip had had two tasks: book the hotel by the airport and arrange the meeting with Dr. Hoffman in Dublin. He'd completed both tasks just before walking out the door.

Thinking back, he worried if sending the book to Brandy had been the right thing to do, but Phillip knew someone had been in his house more than once. Nothing had been taken, but things had been out of place, as if someone had been searching for something. Phillip had the feeling someone knew about the book and desired it. If someone wanted it, it was probably not for anything good. No, the book had needed to go. With him not there, someone would have had time to find its hiding place under the floorboard in his closet, and then the book could have been used for some ungodly purpose.

Socks. Did I pack enough socks?

Ahead, he saw Franky's red hair darting back and forth among the herd of passengers from Flight 309, which had just arrived from Montreal. For the first time, Phillip was having second thoughts about the trip. What business was it of theirs? So what if the nightmare started once again? It was an ocean away, for God's sake. Why must they play a part? Then there was his greatest fear: Would he be able to keep Franky safe? Was he putting him through more than he could endure? Even though

Franky, who was thirty-one years old, had a PhD in literature, and was approaching his tenure at a major university, could hardly be thought of as someone needing a guardian, to Phillip, Franky was his to protect. Phillip had made that promise to his mother at her graveside, and he had every intention of keeping it.

Still, the rationale was there. Only they knew what awaited the unsuspecting population of Ireland. Only they knew the truth about what evil lurked in Banthom House, yet there was no proof they could make a difference. They were not priests, preachers, or rabbis; they had only been unwilling victims. What would they be this time—saviors, killers, hunters of evil with just a touch of vengeance, or simply casualties of an insane demon? They had defeated the evil force once—that much was true—but at such a cost.

The endless causeway gave way to a circular waiting area surrounded by windows that provided a panoramic view of the outside. Evenly spaced were five doorways leading down movable walkways. The one farthest to the right had a check-in counter with a sign for Aer Lingus Flight 201. At last, they had arrived. The flight was on time, and they had twenty minutes to spare—just enough time for a bathroom break and a chance to regroup. Franky had planned everything to a T.

Franky found two open seats in the terminal

and plopped down his backpack. "I've got to go," he said, nodding toward the men's restroom.

"Go. I'll stay with the bags."

Franky was off like a shot. *So that is why he was walking so far ahead*, Phillip thought. Franky was usually gracious enough to walk at the speed of the fifty-three-year-old Phillip, which was not easy for him since Franky generally had only one speed: ninety miles an hour. Not long ago, Phillip had had no problem keeping up with him, but it had gotten to the point where he would just let him go. Franky had seemed to take the hint after a while that Phillip was getting older and had gradually slowed his pace over the years; still, there were times, like that day, when his thoughts were elsewhere.

Phillip set his duffel down on the floor and looked around. There were a few empty seats but not many. He was glad he had talked Franky into first class. The thought of being crammed into the back of a crowed plane for that long of a flight was disheartening. They had a layover in New York, but they did not change planes, so who knew what it would be like the rest of the way. Two rows back, the banshee cry of a newborn came bellowing through the air. "Thank goodness for first class," Phillip said aloud.

Phillip grabbed his duffel to make sure the manuscript was still there. If only someone would believe that the evil was real and that a creature more than two hundred years in the grave could threaten the lives of so many.

Phillip had watched the morning news in terror as the anchors reported the death of James Byrd Jr., an African American who was murdered by three white supremacists in Jasper, Texas. They had dragged him behind a truck, and he'd been killed when his body hit the edge of a culvert, which had decapitated him. The murderers had driven on, dragging his body down the road. Phillips finally had had to turn the TV off. *Evil*, thought Phillip, *comes in many forms.*

Of all the places in the world Brandy Cartwright had thought she would end up in someday, Florida never had been on the list. That was the place old people from the North went when they could no longer deal with cold weather. But there she was, living in a fifty-five-and-older community complete with shuffleboards and tennis courts. Truthfully, she loved every minute of it. It was unobtrusive there, and people left her alone. One could socialize at the clubhouse if he or she sought to, and they had bridge, sewing clubs, tennis clubs, and on and on. Friday was potluck night, and everyone brought a dish. There was an eclectic group of people living there, mostly from the North, including Michigan, Indiana, and New York. Then there were the natural-born Floridians, who, as Brandy had learned early on, did not care and did not want to hear about how much better things were done in the North. Still, everyone there seemed to comprehend that if one chose not to socialize, that was all right too. They did not talk badly about anyone; they were old enough to know that if one desired to be left alone, there was a reason.

Her double-wide was the farthest from the clubhouse. As a matter of fact, she had chosen a lot so far back that there was not another trailer for blocks. The lots were large, and they kept them well groomed. She hoped she would not see a new trailer pop up next to her anytime soon. The farther away from the clubhouse a trailer was, the less the desire to buy was apparent. The area was discreet, with a large retention pond behind her backyard. She would often sit there on a beach chair and fish. The only thing she truly missed was having neighborhood children running around.

She remembered the neighbor boys Franky and Jake back in Parksville, Michigan. When they were small, they'd knocked on her front door in search of handouts, such as cookies and fudge. Their grinning faces had looked up at her with joy and anticipation. The price, which they'd been willing to pay, always had been a big hug. How she'd loved sitting on her front porch while watching them play or ride their bikes. No matter what they'd been doing, they always had taken the time to wave in her direction.

Brandy had a new routine now. In the mornings, she liked to sit on her deck swing on the front lawn while reading her paper. However, the routine was broken that particular day when a UPS truck pulled up in front of her house. A handsome young man got out of the driver's side, dressed in a brown shirt and shorts and holding a brown package.

"Mrs. Cartwright?" he asked as he approached.

Brandy nodded in acknowledgment. She was a bit taken aback, as she could not remember the last time she had received a package.

"Got a special delivery for you. Can you sign here, please?" he said, handing her some paperwork on a clipboard complete with a pen.

"Absolutely," she responded, accepting the clipboard. Hurriedly, she scribbled her signature and then handed the clipboard back to the nice young man.

"Must be something special if they overnighted it and insured it like this," he said, retrieving the paperwork. "Have a blessed day, ma'am," he added with a smile.

"You too, dear," she responded. It was nice to see young people with good manners.

An envelope was taped on top of the package. She opened it, and seeing the sender's name put a smile on her face. The package was from a dear friend in Parksville, Michigan: Phillip Parker. As she pored over the note, however, her mood rapidly changed. As she looked down at the package wrapped in plain brown paper and tied with a string, a touch of sadness overcame her as memories of Parksville came roaring back in waves of happiness and sorrow. She recalled the love of people she had known and the evil that had taken them away.

As spelled out in Phillip's letter, her task was easy enough: put the package in a safe place, and leave it there. He had specifically asked that she not open it, as the exceptional item he was entrusting to her was very old and valuable. He and Franky were traveling out of the county and wanted the item in safe hands until they returned. Brandy bought none of it. The package had to do with what had occurred in Parksville many years ago; she could feel it right down to her very bones. Usually, letters from Franky or Phillip left her in a good place, but this one left a feeling of dread. She knew the matter was not over, whatever it was, and the thing sitting in her lap, for good or evil, would play an enormous part. Why she felt that way, she was not sure—maybe because since the day she'd learned the truth, she'd known the battle had not ended.

Franky had chosen to tell her everything that had taken place back in Parksville—all of his struggles, all of his loss, and all of his terror—and for that, she was grateful. She also knew she was one of the select few who knew the truth, and they had never breathed a word of it to the police.

Brandy knew there were a number of obvious reasons for not telling their story to anyone else. Why risk telling a story that would implicate them in the deaths of many, and who would have believed them anyway? She had refused to believe the bullshit laid down by the police as to what really had happened. Maybe it was because she and Franky had such a special bond that she knew deep down that Franky and Phillip had seen the whole thing unfold. They forgot that she too had felt the presence of the foul creature. One thing was certain: they were both emotionally torn apart. There might have been a million reasons for not telling everything, and that was their business, but she thanked God she was there to help when they needed it the most. Two purer souls she had never met.

On the first anniversary of his mother's death, Franky had come to her and told his horrific story through a torrent of tears, his body shaking to the point that Brandy had had to hold him tightly in her arms. He'd explained that they had discovered a witch living among them, and it had killed his cousin Jake right in front of his eyes. Franky had found his mother torn apart in the attic of an old mansion, and he told of the battle of life and death he and Phillip had fought. That battle had taken the lives of a priest and Phillip's good friend Kip Gillmore. He'd disclosed to her every painful detail. It had seemed a great relief for him, as if just letting someone else know what they had gone through was cleansing. As Brandy had embraced him in her arms, she'd vowed to never tell a soul, and she'd kept her word.

In some ways, it seemed a lifetime ago, and in others, it seemed as if it had happened just yesterday. Brandy got up and walked toward the double-wide with the package in tow. She would do what was asked of her and put it in a safe place. The mood to read the paper was gone—it would have been bad news anyway, she was sure. Maybe it was the letter, or maybe it was just a sense of nostalgia, but for whatever reason, for the first time in her life, she truly felt alone.

It ended up being a two-hour flight from Detroit to New York. The plane hit air pocket after air pocket, and at times, the flight resembled a roller-coaster ride. Franky was hoping to take a short nap; unlike

Phillip, he had not had an easy night. Every time he dozed off, he would find himself drifting back to Parksville—back to the manor's dark attic. His arms were tied, and the smell of rotting flesh was in the air. The top half of his mother's mutilated dead body was creeping out of an old, dilapidated trunk. He could see clearly her bluish complexion and hear the thump her upper torso made when it collided with the floor. He saw the blood trailing as she scuttled toward him with a look of anguish in her eyes. The creature Fritz had made him see awful, vile, evil things. It had taken him years to get the visions out of his head, and now they had started invading his dreams once again. It was obvious why with their pending expedition, but that did not make it any less oppressive. If it had not been for Phillip and Mrs. Cartwright, he would have ended up in some deprived home for the insane. He hoped matters would not get that ruthless this time.

He tried to read, but the bouncing of the plane made it impossible, so for most of the trip, he sat lost in thought about what would take place once they landed in Dublin. He and Phillip had gone over everything a hundred times, but still, they might have left something unsaid or undone.

They landed in New York amid a barrage of lightning and thunder. Franky was sure the flight would be diverted, but down it came, and to his amazement, it was one of softest landings he could remember. By the time passengers had shuffled off and new ones had loaded, the weather had started to clear. Once they were back in the air, the sun was bright, and the flight was as smooth as one could hope. *Just another seven hours*, thought Franky. There was a five-hour time difference between Dublin and Detroit, and they had left with an eight o'clock departure that morning and, with the layover, were scheduled to land in Dublin at eleven thirty that night, Dublin time. First class or not, he would be glad to get there. This was not his first European adventure; he had been to London twice and Paris once. All three trips had been for research, with just a little craziness thrown in. He had never traveled farther than Grand Rapids with Phillip, so this trip was going to be something new. Over the years, they had become good friends—almost family, in a way. Their two-decade age difference did not seem to make much difference to either one of them. Yes, sometimes when Franky was younger, Phillip had taken on a father-knows-best mentality, but Franky never had taken it in a bad way. After all they had been through, Phillip's concern was somewhat heartening during those early years. As the years had gone by, Phillip had put that mentality behind him, but still, to that day, in his own way, he was protective of Franky. That thought gave Franky comfort.

It was not going to be easy to tell Phillip he had taken a new position at the University of Michigan. Sure, it was only an hour up Highway 94, but still, they would not be together, and that would be something new for them. However, it was time for Franky to find that certain someone in his life. He had dated some of his coworkers at the college but never had felt any connection with any of them, and none of them had with him either. When he was younger, he had never even considered the thought of settling down and enjoying the companionship of a single woman for the rest of his life. He'd wanted to be free to experience life and all it had to offer. All of that had seemed to change when he reached thirty. He'd started pondering family, what legacy he would leave behind, and what the impending years would hold for him. One thing was certain: the answer was not in Parksville.

First, however, they had to finish that adventure. Franky had made up his mind that regardless of what Phillip had in mind, he was going to make sure they did not get too close to the fire. Franky had lost enough, and he was not about to lose any more. With any luck, Dr. Hoffman would lead the offense, with him and Phillip on the sidelines, sending in signals.

Outside the window, the sun was shining brightly. Franky looked out and saw nothing but ocean. He was hoping to get glimpse of Greenland or Iceland—something—but all he had seen for the past three hours was open water. Next to him, Phillip sat studying the old manuscript written by a witch-hunting priest in the 1800s. That manuscript had led them to the truth about the witch Fritz, who'd terrorized them in Parksville, and Phillip now studied it to learn about Banthom of Dublin, the witch who'd schooled Fritz in the occult. His body, like that of Fritz, never had been found, and now it seemed he too had returned from the grave.

"Anything new?" Franky asked, turning to face Phillip.

"Not really," Phillip replied, closing the book and placing it back on his lap. "I was just going back over the list of items the priest said he needed to fight a witch."

Franky knew the list by heart because Phillip had repeated it a hundred times over the years. "A Bible, a crucifix, holy water, rope, flint, hemlock, sage, and salt," Franky replied.

"Yes, I know I am driving you crazy with this. It's just that I get the religious symbolism for most of the items, even if I am not sure how they are supposed to be used, but the hemlock? The salt I get as well. What witch story doesn't include salt? But the hemlock—I don't get it." Phillip shook his head. "Father McDonald was vague in so many places. He says very little about the time he spent with the cult in London, and he says very little about Banthom or Dublin, mentioning them almost as if in passing. He talks a lot about hunting down the cult, tracking Fritz to the new world, and building his church, but I don't know. It's like he's only telling half the story."

"Maybe he is vague for a reason," Franky said.

"But why? I mean, if he wanted those in the church to kill the witch if it returned, why be vague?"

"Think about it. If he said too much about what it takes to become a witch—" Franky gave a quick peek around to make sure no one was paying attention. "I mean, that kind of knowledge may be best guarded. Don't you think? A warning, yes, but a guidebook?"

"Point taken. Still, it seems so broken, like tidbits of a journal," Phillip said.

"Maybe he gave the missing parts to someone he knew he could trust—another priest maybe. We know little about the man before he started the manuscript, and we are not even sure he was from Dublin. We know he had just taken charge of a church when he heard about Banthom. It says so right there," said Franky, pointing to the manuscript.

"Are you suggesting McDonald went there to find Banthom?"

"Think about it. He knew a lot about witches before he ever left for London."

"True, but McDonald said he didn't even know Banthom when he got there."

"Maybe Banthom wasn't the one he was after. Who knows? Maybe Banthom was converted. I don't know. I just feel like the priest was summoned to Dublin—like he was sent there for a specific reason," Franky said, and then he glanced out the window.

"Maybe this Dr. Hoffman has some answers." Phillip spoke with a tone of uncertainty. He had been nervous the day before when he'd pulled out his little black address book to make the call. The man's credentials were impressive, but the phone call he'd placed to the good doctor had been somewhat disheartening. Phillip had called with the premise that he and Franky had read about the story and were interested in researching the location. Dr. Hoffman never had asked why they would be following the English tabloids or why they had an interest in visiting the site of the gruesome murders. He was more interested in how they knew of him. Phillip had explained they had read his study on the connections among mythology, psychology, and parapsychology and found him insightful. He'd failed to comment on the research they had conducted for years to find a comrade in arms in case Banthom emerged from his unholy grave. They already knew that Hoffman was well known in his other chosen field, and they had read about many of his investigations. They also knew he had tried to get a chance to investigate Banthom House on numerous occasions and had been denied by its current owner.

After playing to Hoffman's ego for a few minutes, Phillip had asked for a meeting.

"You want to come all the way to Dublin to visit the location?" Hoffman had asked a little too enthusiastically.

"Why, yes, that is our intention."

"When are you going to be here?"

"We are actually getting ready to leave in a few minutes."

"I will set something up for the morning."

With that, Hoffman had given him his home number, which Phillip had written down at once in his little black address book. Hoffman had asked that they call when they landed, and he would give a time and location for them to meet. It had been as if Hoffman could not wait to get off the phone.

Phillip put his hand on Franky's arm. "After all, he has been working hard to get into Banthom House."

"Yeah, maybe," replied Franky half-heartedly.

Phillip stuck his hand in the breast pocket of his suit coat, checking to make sure something was there. Franky knew what he was checking for:

his little black book in which he kept every phone number he'd ever had. Phillip kept it with him always. Franky had tried buying a new one for him for his birthday last year, but he'd been unable to find one; no one used them anymore. As for Franky, all his numbers were on his Motorola Star cell. If it died, he would be lost. Maybe sometimes the old ways were the best.

Twelve-year-old Annie Nash threw her large red duffel bag out her bedroom window before she stuck her head out, looking left and then right to make sure the coast was clear. Then she clambered out herself. The night sky was clear, and the moon was half full; still, she felt exposed in its light. It was too easy to be seen. This was it; she was leaving and never coming back. If she could make her way to the coast, she could find a way to her grandma's house. She was almost certain Grandma's house would not offer her sanctuary because she had pleaded for ages to move in with her with no success. She understood Grandma would just call her mom to come collect her. But what her grandmother's house did offer was cash—cold, hard euros in hand. The old woman did not have a fortune stuck in her mattress, but there was a nice stash in the cookie jar in the kitchen—Annie had seen it. She had seen her grandmother pull the jar down from the top shelf and stick a large wad of cash in it when she thought no one was looking. She remembered Grandma saying more than once to her mom that it was important to put a bit of quid away for a rainy day. *Well, Grandma, it's pouring now.*

Annie heard a sound from somewhere in the house and stopped dead in her tracks. If her mom caught her, she would get a thrashing for sure. After a few minutes, she decided it was safe to move forward. With her bedroom in the back of the house, she would have to go under the bathroom window; past her mom's window, which her mom always kept open at night; and then past the front of the house to reach the road.

Her mom was probably passed out drunk, which was nothing new; her new man, Gary, on the other hand, was often up late at night. The pig was a bum with no intention of going to work, and Annie was sure her mom knew it. Annie hated him with a passion. Since the night her mom first had brought him home, Annie had known there was something peculiar about him and the way he scrutinized her when he thought no one else was looking. Once, she had caught him peering through the bathroom window from outside when she was taking a bath. That had creeped her out so badly she had started bathing with her bathing suit on. Whenever her mom was absent, he would be near, watching.

During most the day, when her mom was away tending bar at the local pub, he would stroll around the house in nothing more than his tiny, skintight briefs. At least once a day, she would see him sitting on the couch, pulling on his thing over and over until it got stiff. Then he would purposely parade around in front of her, making sure she could see everything and acting as if none of it was really happening. That display was often followed by a trip to the bathroom, where she would hear him grunt and moan from behind the door. She knew what the sicko was doing; she wasn't stupid.

In the middle of the night, he would walk around in the house with nothing on. Annie knew that because more than once, she had caught him lurking outside her bedroom door, peering in and pulling on his thing. Last night, however, had been the straw that broke the camel's back. As she had lain sleeping, she'd felt something caressing her leg. It had started at her ankle and then moved up toward her private parts. She'd shrieked in terror, and sitting up, she'd seen his furry naked ass dashing out the door.

"You all right, honey?" her mother's half-sleeping voice had asked from her bedroom.

"She's fine. I thought I heard something and went in to check on her. Scared her is all. Go back to sleep," Gary had replied. Then she'd heard their bedroom door close.

The next morning, she'd told her mom all about the frightening experience, but her mom had acted as if it were no big deal and said, "He would never do anything to hurt you, honey. He was just checking on you." Annie had gone on to tell her about the bathroom, the daily stiffy shows, and the night visits to her bedroom doorway.

"Dammit, Annie, don't start that shit with me. He is a good man. I know he strolls around in his underwear at home—most men do. Don't you spoil this for me. I am happier than I have been in years. I'll talk to him about wearing pants around the house, okay?"

Annie had turned and run away before her mom could say another word. Upon reaching her bedroom door, she'd slammed it shut and, for the first time in her life, locked it. Her mom had followed right behind. No sooner had the door closed than her mom had been pounding on it. "Unlock this fucking door!" she'd demanded.

Annie had sat on her bed, hugging a stuffed panda bear and crying. Why she had bothered to tell her mother was beyond her. She had known her mom would take his side; she did it with all her boyfriends.

"Dammit, Annie, let me in! Don't be such a little cunt."

"Go away! I hate you!" Annie had shouted.

"You're lucky I'm late for work. You just wait until I get home," her mother had said, and with that, Annie had heard her stomp away.

That night, Annie had avoided them both. She'd stayed in her bedroom, packing and planning. She'd heard them out in the living room with music blaring, laughing and talking loudly. They were drunk, as usual, so she knew it was only a matter of time before they passed out.

The bathroom window was no problem because it was higher than she was tall, but at her mother's bedroom window, she had to crouch as low as she could and silently move forward. All her senses heightened. She hoped the top of her head could not be seen. She heard movement on her mom's squeaky bed. Once again, she stopped dead in her tracks. Someone was getting up; she could hear the bedroom door open. Annie was breathing so hard she was afraid they would be able to hear her from inside the house through the open window, and her heart was pounding. From behind came light from the bathroom window. Slowly, she moved forward, dragging her large bag behind her. She was not sure if someone looking out the bathroom window could see, but she knew that if it was him, he might want to make a stop in her room for God knew what, and if she was gone, then what? She was just at the edge of the window, when the bathroom light went off, and she heard her mom's bedroom door swing shut once again.

She started inching along, and once past the window, she stood and ran, looking over her shoulder to make sure no further lights came on as she went. She almost fell as her feet hit the hard road, but she kept her footing. She did not slow her pace until she was a full two blocks from the house. The night air was cool and crisp, and she wondered if she should have brought her winter coat. For the first time in months, she felt relief. Even though she had no place to go, no family she could run to, and no idea how she was going to make it on her own, she felt better. With her grandma's unwilling contribution, she would find some way of making it. Maybe she would buy a ticket to London; they would never find her there.

Ahead in the distance, she saw a dark figure making its way up the road along the sidewalk on the opposite side. Fright rose in her. She was not one to easily be scared, but for some reason, seeing another person did not seem right that late at night in that neighborhood. Annie stopped, and the thought of returning home crossed her mind for a moment. She could have sneaked back in through her window with no one the wiser, but her confidence started to build back up, and she pressed on. Her fears soon waned as the figure made a sudden turn to the right on the road just ahead. *Thank goodness.* She would have to get tough if she was going to make it on her own, dammit.

It would only take a couple hours to reach her grandma's house—she knew because her mom had once made her walk home. She had told her mom she would rather walk home than ride with her, as drunk as she was, so her mom had said fine, stopped the car, and made her walk the entire way by herself. She'd been only ten years old at the time. Her mom had been between boyfriends then, and that usually made matters worse between them; she drank more when she was by herself. It had been the middle of the day, but how alone and afraid she had felt. She'd been sure her mom was watching her from somewhere that day, waiting for her to plead for a ride and show how wrong she'd been to question her, but Annie had refused to give in and had managed to walk all the way. When she'd gotten home, she'd found her mom passed out on the sofa. She had not been watching. She had not been making sure Annie made it home. That had been a new day for her and her mom's relationship. Annie never had felt truly loved again.

Finally, at the end of the hill and the end of her road, she crossed Route 119 and started following the train tracks along the shoreline. She knew they came out right where she needed to turn on Strathmore and thought it best to stay away from the road in case they came looking for her. She knew it was a long walk, and the last time, she'd not been carrying everything she owned on her back. It was dark and quiet; the only sound was of the waves hitting the rocky shoreline. As she walked, she stopped periodically, picked up a handful of stones, and threw them one at a time down the never-ending tracks, imagining Gary's face in front of her each time. She was just letting off a good one, when something came bursting out of the bushes right in front of her. Annie let out a high-pitched scream.

In front of her feet, a rabbit stopped, lifted itself onto its hind legs, and looked around.

Dammit, Mr. Bunny, you scared me half to death. The rabbit scampered off in a dead run, leaving Annie a little shaken. That was when she first noticed the rancid odor. Annie looked around to see if she had just walked past something dead along the tracks. The smell reeked so badly it was making her sick to her stomach; she bent over and laid down her duffel bag, waiting for the feeling to pass. That was why she never saw it coming at her out of the night—the dark figure of a man. Before she knew what had happened, its ice-cold hand was over her mouth, holding her so tightly she couldn't scream. With its other arm, she felt it grab her around the waist. With little effort, it started to drag her off into the darkness toward the sea.

The people of Dublin knew little about the Burk estate. The first known records of the estate were in the thirteenth century, but then the estate was an abandoned castle with no records showing who, if anyone, occupied it. Some believed it might have been the summer place for Dublin Castle. Such locations were common during that time throughout Europe, as the smell of animal and human waste became too overbearing during summer months. While no one knew exactly, it gave many of the locals a good tale to tell. In the fifteenth century, the castle was in ruins. It was eventually purchased by the Burk family, who in turn leased it to the British crown. The outer walls remained intact, but everything within them was removed—all except the dungeon, which housed some of the oldest artifacts ever discovered in the area. The artifacts would become the property of the Burk family and remain as a private collection. What was later to become the Burk estate, built directly over the dungeon, began as barracks for British troops dating back to the early sixteenth century. Many of the locals speculated that Bloody Mary housed troops in hiding to reinstate Catholic rule in England, and after the reign of Queen Mary, Queen Elizabeth used the private dungeon below the barracks to quietly contain Catholic supporters in her push to reestablish the Church of England. That was never proven, of course, but it too made for a good story. The Burk family regained control of the land in 1608 and converted the barracks into a lush estate. They tore down all the outer stone walls and opened up the land with gardens and sloping lawns.

The property's current owner, Benjamin Burk, a wealthy young aristocrat whose family was known for being private and almost reclusive, had just returned from a trip abroad when word of the killings at Banthom House reached his ears. It was all over the news and in the daily paper. It had been more than two weeks since the killings, and Benjamin knew he might already be too late to prepare. He had to make the house safe against the imminent doom that would follow. His entire staff was gone; he had sent them all on holiday, which was not unusual for the eccentric man. His outward demeanor seemed harsh at times, but his staff knew him as an overly giving individual who overindulged the people he cared about, including his staff. He was quick to hire and fire, but if he liked a person, he kept him or her as long as he could and treated him or her more as family than help.

Up the winding stairway he went, carrying a large container of salt. It was hard to believe that after all that time, the prophecies of his aristocratic, stuffed-shirt family tree had come true. The witch had returned, just as his father had told him he would someday. It was now his duty to guard the family's secret past and bring an end to the ghastly tale. That was his legacy, his gift from multiple generations of Burk.

On the fourth floor, he made a rapid turn to the left and walked to the end of the hall, where the attic door was. *Too many windows in the attic to contend with*, he thought, and he simply laid a straight line of salt on the floor beneath the door. If the witch got into the attic, at least he could not pass beyond that point. Benjamin turned and looked down the long corridor. It had been years since he had been on the third floor. That section of the house was seldom used. Unlike the rest of the house, that segment had kept its barracks-like appearance through the years. Rows of doors, twelve on one side and eleven on the other, lined the walls. Each door was spaced the same distance apart, and behind each, he would find the same sized room, with one window directly in the middle of the far wall. *This shit is going to take all night,* he thought. "That's what I get for staying in this overdone mausoleum," he said to the open air.

When his parent had passed away—both from unhealthy habits, Mom the smoking and Dad the booze—Benjamin had been left with the entire family estate. He had no siblings, aunts, or uncles to squabble with; it was just him. By the age of thirty, he'd been one of the richest men in all of Ireland. Money came with its own burdens, however, as he'd learned early on.

After entering the first door and turning on the overhead light, he wasted no time in hiking directly to the large, square window and laying down a thick line of salt, making damn sure that every inch of the seal was coated. He took a moment to gaze out into the moonlight. He remembered when he was young and his parents were both healthy. Then they were content and, for the most part, happy. Before they became ill, his parents would have grand parties, and all the rooms on that floor would be filled with guests. They would come for the festivities on Friday night, and usually, the last of them would leave Sunday morning. Back then, the house was full of music and laughter, but that seemed like a lifetime ago. No one other than a Burk or the staff had entered that part of the house in more than ten years. Every day the staff would clean. They changed the sheets on all the beds in all the rooms monthly and shampooed the carpets and washed the windows every spring. Benjamin turned and walked out, turning off the light behind him. *What a waste*, he thought.

CHAPTER 2

A GATHERING OF STRANGERS

Mary Todd sat in the corner of the room, taking in the odd collection of individuals sitting around Dr. Hoffman's living room. The girl sitting next to her on the ottoman wore a flowered dress—daisies, of all things. She resembled a young Mia Farrow with her slender frame, except she had dark brown hair and bright hazel eyes. With a good breeze, she would have been gone—no competition from that one. Next to the girl on the ottoman sat a heavyset Oriental man in a chair. He appeared to be in his midtwenties and was dressed in a suit and tie. He was boring—she could tell he was a loser lost in some time warp of the 1970s.

Standing by the door was a tall blond who sported a surfer-dude appearance. Mary eyed him.

He had a hard, great body and tight pants with a nice bulge. His shirt was unbuttoned just enough to show a hairy chest. He was definitely on her hit list.

Across the room, sitting on the overstuffed couch, was an older gentleman—midfifties maybe. He was eye candy as well but not at the top of her list for the moment. Next to him sat a redhead. She had watched him walk in, glancing at his tight ass right from the start. He had a slender build, looked to be in his late twenties or early thirties, and was wearing jeans as well. She had not gotten a peek at his package but was sure it was a nice one. There was no doubt: the choice was between the blond and the redhead. She would do them both, of course; it was just a matter of which heart she wanted to break first. She turned to the redhead sitting on the couch and gave him her patented come-hither smile.

Hoffman had asked them all to be there at eight o'clock. Why so early was beyond her, but each had been prompt in arrival except for Hoffman himself, who'd said he had an errand to run but would be back in plenty of time. He was now a full fifteen minutes late. It was obviously awkward for everyone, as it seemed not one person other than the two men on the couch, who'd come in together, knew anyone else. They had offered each other smiles across the room, but no one seemed to know what to say. Mary stood up. She thought at least she would go around the room and let them introduce themselves. "I am sorry about Dr. Hoffman's lateness, but I am sure he will be here shortly. In the meantime—"

All of a sudden, Hoffman came bounding through the front door. He was huffing and puffing as if he had just finished a morning marathon through the streets of Dublin. He placed a large briefcase on the floor by the door, next to the blond, and walked to the center of the room.

"Sorry for being late. I hope you all have made yourselves comfortable."

Mary, still standing, helped him off with his coat. She was glad he was there to take charge of the situation.

Hoffman immediately walked over to the redhead sitting on the couch. "Dr. Lake, I presume?" He offered his hand.

"Franky," the redhead responded as he shook hands. "And this is Dr. Parker," he added, gesturing to his right.

The other man stood, offering his hand as well. "Phillip," he said.

Mary was taken aback by the exchange. Dr. Hoffman would never have let someone call him by his first name. The two Americans seemed far less formal than any of the intellectuals she had encountered in Dublin.

"We are ever so pleased to have you here and so glad for your interest in the Banthom estate," Hoffman said, never offering his first name in kind. "I am sure you are wondering why I have invited all these nice young people to our meeting. You see, I am planning an investigation of Banthom House. Current situations being as they are, the current owner will undoubtedly consent, as it has been a passion of mine for some time." He seemed to fall into deep thought, and a short pause ensued. "Perhaps introductions are in order." He turned and put his hand on Mary's shoulder. "This is Mary Todd, a student of mine who has agreed to work as my secretary for the duration of this little adventure."

Mary smiled, even though the thought of his touch made her uneasy. She had agreed to the assignment because she needed the money; she had no real like for Dr. Hoffman and his crass manner. Still, she had worked for worse, and the job was not difficult from what Hoffman had told her. It would involve a lot of research, which she liked doing anyway. That day's task was simply to get them all there and feed them. Hoffman had said he would fill her in and enlighten her on everything needing done when the investigation started. Somehow, she felt he himself was somewhat unsure of what that entailed.

"On the ottoman is Josette Bradley. Josette is a

world-renowned medium from London. She has agreed to offer her unique talents." Josette did not rise but offered a bashful smile to the group.

A medium? Do people still believe in that bullshit? Mary thought to herself. Most of them were just scam artists taking money from little old ladies who wanted to talk to their dead husbands.

"Next to her is Joe Chung. He is also a student of mine. He is an electronics wizard and will be helping me with all our neat little gadgets."

Joe stood with a huge smile and gave a small nod.

Mary bit her lip to suppress a giggle. *How stereotypical can you get?* The nod was one inch short of a bow, and worse yet, he had a cheesy smile.

"This," he said, pointing to the blond, "is Shawn Davis. Shawn comes to us from sunny California, where I worked with him on another project. It just so happened he was in town doing a shoot for the BBC. He will be our cameraman."

Shawn walked over to where the two American men stood. "Pleasure to meet you," he said to Phillip, offering his hand, and then he did the same to Franky. "How was your flight?"

"Long," responded Franky with a grin.

With the ice broken, everyone stood and started sharing greetings. Out of the corner of her eye, Mary caught the two American professors whispering to each other. She was not sure what they had expected at the meeting, but the looks on their faces made it clear this was not it.

"Is everything ready, Mary?" Hoffman said with a small smile.

"Yes. Please, everyone, come this way into the dining room. We have a breakfast prepared," responded Mary, giving a wave of her hand toward the kitchen. "Through the kitchen and on your right."

"We will start laying down the game plans over some eggs Benedict I had delivered from a quaint little café around the corner," Hoffman said.

As everyone was making his or her way to the dining room, Mary saw Phillip grab Hoffman by the arm. "Please, can we talk alone for just a moment?" he asked.

In the early morning light, a large black cat jumped onto the windowsill of Maggie Nash's open bedroom window. It sat staring in at the two figures that lay in the bed just a foot away. The man slept with his mouth wide open, snoring. The woman was on her side with her head buried under the blankets. The cat leaped the short distance to the bed with a soft landing. Slowly, it crept over the legs of the sleeping woman, over one leg at a time of the man, and up the far side of the bed. Inches away from the man's face, it paused nonchalantly, looking around for any sign of life from the two drowsing slugs in the bed. There was not a sound. Slowly, it crouched like a lion before the lurch, its claws extended, and then leaped. Within a split second, it hit its mark squarely on the man's face, where it started clawing feverishly at his eyes with its front claws while using its back claws on his lower lip. At once, the man grabbed the cat and hurled it across the room, where it landed hard against the wall. The damage, however, had already been done. Disoriented and screaming in pain, the man rolled over onto the floor with a loud thud.

"Gary! Gary, are you okay?" the now-awake Maggie said. She looked over to find him lying on the floor and covering his eyes. "What the hell happened?"

"Fuck, this hurts," he mournfully replied.

"Let me see," she said, grabbing him by both arms and pulling his upper body onto the bed. She could see blood gushing from his lower lip. It looked as if someone had taken a razor to it. He still had his eyes covered with his large hands. She grabbed his arms and pulled his hands down. His eyes were even worse than his lip. "Open your eyes, and let me see."

"I can't open my fucking eyes!" he yelled.

The cat, which had landed on its feet, looked

no worse for wear. It sat quietly watching the interaction taking place and looking for the next target, which didn't take long. Gary was on his knees and bent over the bed with his legs apart, and the cat spotted his hanging fruit completely exposed. The cat once again pounced, but this time, it led with its teeth. It planted them deep into the empty sack above the hanging testicles and at once started clawing upward with both front and back claws. In shock, Gary stood up, but the hold the cat had on him was so strong the cat rose with him, hanging between his legs and digging deeper and deeper into his nut sack. Gary reached down to grab the cat, but it seemed to sense his move; it let go and ran to the other side of room, hissing with its back hunched.

Maggie, who had seen the whole thing unfold, sat up in bed and pulled the covers up to her neck. "What the hell is happening? It must have rabies!"

Gary, who was still trying to get a grip on the situation, tried to open his eyes. The pain was unbearable, but he finally forced them open just enough to see a hazy fog, an outline of furniture, and the black mass that was running toward him.

This time, the cat ran right up his leg. Gary swung, but once again, the cat avoided the blow by shooting out of the way just in time. Gary turned to see where the attack would come next. As he did, the cat jumped onto the bed and then directly at his chest. Gary backed up to avoid the onslaught but tripped over his own feet and fell. The back of his head hit the dresser with such force that it made his chin smack against his chest before he landed hard on the floor. The cat walked over and gave him a final scratch on the nose to let him know it had won.

Maggie was petrified. Slowly, the cat walked across the room and then hopped onto the bed. It walked up the entire length of her quivering body and stopped just short of touching Maggie's nose with its nose. It stood there for a moment, staring into her eyes; arched its back; put its ears back; bared its teeth; and let out a long, unnerving hiss. Maggie could do nothing. She felt her bladder release. After what seemed an eternity to Maggie, the cat turned, hopped onto the window ledge, lifted its tail, and sprayed. It turned once more, looked Maggie straight in the eyes, and then jumped down and was gone.

Overcoming her fear, Maggie jumped out of bed and ran to Gary. His body was twitching queerly, and she lifted his head to place it under her arm only to feel a large indent in the back of his skull. "Annie!" she yelled. "Annie, come here! I need you. I need your help. For God's sake, Annie." All of a sudden, Gary's shaking stopped, and he let out a soft gasp of air. She could feel his body go limp in her arms. "Annie, please! Please come help me, honey! I need you!" Maggie yelled, but there was no response.

"Thank you for meeting with me alone," said Phillip, entering the makeshift office. The bifold closet doors on the north wall gave way to the fact that this was a bedroom being put to better use by his blustering host. Shelves of books lined the walls, an old TV with a VCR recorder on top sat in the corner under a small window, and along the south wall was his desk.

"Not a problem," responded Dr. Hoffman, motioning to a chair in front of his desk. "I am sorry for springing the entire team on you at once; I just thought it best for everyone to start on the same page."

After taking his seat and waiting for Dr. Hoffman to do the same, Phillip continued. "I would be remiss if I failed to warn you about the danger you and your team may well encounter."

"Professor Parker, investigating Banthom House comes with certain danger, which I think is apparent to us all. I mean, those kids—it was terrible."

"You think there is a maniac on the loose, don't you? Some devil cult looking for blood sacrifice? Maybe someone trying to raise the unholy spirit of Banthom himself?"

Hoffman looked at him, trying not to show his curiosity. "Well, yes, that is what I believe happened. Are you saying I am wrong in this matter?"

Phillip took a long pause and looked into Hoffman's eyes. He was trying to read him, to see what impact his gruesome acknowledgment would have on him. There was nothing there; the man had a poker face that Al Capone would have admired. There was nothing to do but just blurt it out and see what effect it had on him. "Did you know that Banthom had an associate by the name of Fritz?"

"Never heard of him," Hoffman replied, leaning in toward Phillip.

"Did you know that Banthom was a Satanist?"

"Yes, that is common knowledge, Professor Parker," he replied, still being polite.

"Did you know he was a witch?"

"I heard that he practiced the black arts, yes."

"He did more than practice," Phillip said, and then he took another long pause, looking for the right way to put it.

"For God's sake, man, just say what it is you want to say," Hoffman said at last, knowing Phillip was building up to something. He was getting impatient.

"Okay, here it goes. Banthom was putting together a cult when he died—a cult of witches.

Professor Lake and I encountered one of his cult members in Michigan. His name was Fritz. I don't know if that was a first or last name; I know only that he was one mean son of a bitch."

"Well," Hoffman said with half a nervous chuckle.

"I know it sounds crazy, but the man had been buried alive all those years. He was a witch, Dr. Hoffman. A real live witch."

Hoffman did not say a word. He got up and, rubbing his chin, walked behind his chair, lost in thought.

Now it was Phillip who started to get impatient. He shifted in his chair as Hoffman paced.

"Professor, I have seen a lot of things, traveled to many places, and done many investigations, and one thing I know for sure is that if a man of your stature and education can sit here after traveling halfway around the world and tell me he has faced a witch, then I believe there may be some validity in what he is saying."

"Thank God. It may just save your life," Phillip replied a little too loudly.

"So this Fritz—do you think he is the one who tried to raise Banthom?"

"Fritz is dead. He died the only way these things can be killed: with flame and prayer."

"You mean to say—"

"Yes, my good doctor. It was Banthom who

killed the two children," Phillip said as he stood. "And he will take more lives before this is over. Fritz killed eleven people in just a few short days. He ate them alive, just like the girl found in Banthom House. They need to feed; it's what makes them whole again, if you know what I mean. I am going to leave you with this. It is the manuscript of a priest who tells of his own encounters with Banthom and Fritz, only it happened more than two hundred years ago." With that, Phillip pulled out the manuscript from his briefcase. He was taking a risk, he knew, but Hoffman had to know the whole truth. "Once you have finished this, I will tell you about our own encounter with the beast."

"Please, there is no need. Put that thing back in your pack. I am not going to lie to you, Professor. I brought you here in hopes of getting you to fund this investigation. I still need you to do so. We both know the house must be investigated. I know the current owner shares in your belief of witches and such, and I will need your help to convince him to give me access."

"Professor Lake and I will fully fund the investigation as long as we tell the others what they might face in that house. I will not put their lives in jeopardy without their knowing the risks," Phillip said.

"Nor would I, Professor Parker. Nor would I,"

said Hoffman. "But let's wait until we speak to the owner and see if he will give us permission before we even start telling this tale to the others. Then we'll take it from there."

"You don't believe a word I am saying, do you?" said Phillip with a sigh as he sat back down hard in his chair. "I guess I wouldn't believe it myself if the tables were turned."

"Well, it seems to me that if this monster was loose, it would be all over the news. I mean, there would be half-eaten bodies all over Dublin, don't you think?"

"I don't know. Maybe this one is smarter than the last one, taking his time and hiding the bodies. I don't know, but you must believe me. He is out there, and he will kill whoever stands in his way."

"Mr. Parker, I believe that you believe, and you will have to be satisfied with that for now if we want to move forward. If permission is given to investigate the house, then I will let you tell everyone your tale from start to finish, but for now, let's go enjoy our breakfast. Then we will drive out to see the current owner of the estate. Deal?"

"Deal," Phillip said, somewhat unsatisfied. On the way back to join the others, Phillip had the strangest feeling it was not the first time Hoffman had heard the story. Something about the way he'd reacted—so matter-of-factly—was odd. *He did not even want to look at the manuscript. Why?*

Down the street and two blocks to the east of the Nash home, Mathew Duryee walked in the afternoon sun. He checked his tie, pants, and belt, making sure all was in place. This was the biggest deal of his life, and it involved some real badasses. They were the kind of people who, if the deal fell through, would leave him at the bottom of the bay with cement for tennis shoes. Just a block up the street sat a five-million-dollar payday that would end his career. They'd had a quick meeting, and he'd received half the payment up front. He'd receive the last half after the deed was accomplished. Then he could be off to the islands.

Mathew made a living in a particularly dangerous way: he killed people for enormous amounts money. He was good at it because he made it personal. Big money came with certain requests, messages left for those who might cross any employers in the future. Mathew had cut off more body parts and stuffed them in more orifices than he cared to remember. He preferred his knife to a gun. Guns were loud, and there was no suspense; a knife got him up close and personal. He could feel the life drain from his victims like air from a punctured tire. When he worked with women, he always broke their necks. He'd never cared for taking a knife to a woman. Maybe he was sentimental, but he liked to kill them quickly.

Murder had no meaning for him—it never

had. When he'd been just thirteen, he'd visited his cousin just outside of Toronto. He'd enjoyed the flight, his aunt and uncle, and everything to do with his vacation—except for his cousin Tad. Tad was a loud, fat, spoiled bully. Maybe that was why Mathew had killed him. Mathew remembered it as if it were yesterday.

It was still early morning when his cousin convinced Mathew to join him for a walk. He knew Tad wanted to leave before his parents got up so he could smoke his early morning cigarette, a routine he had followed every day since Mathew had arrived. They left through the back door and walked across the modest-sized backyard. At the far end was a trail into a thickly wooded area. That was where they went every morning so Tad could puff his cancer stick. Mathew made his way to a log where he had sat a few times to wait until Tad was done, but that time, Tad kept going. The path came out near a busy overpass not half a mile from their house. In the week they had been there, Mathew had seen a total of only maybe five cars traveling down the road. There were no exit ramps from the busy highway, and other than his aunt and uncle's house, there was nothing but farmland to be seen for miles. When they got to the overpass, Mathew and Tad looked over the edge at the cars flying by underneath them. Both tried to spit just in time to see it hit the cars below.

For the first time, he was enjoying Tad's company, but the feeling was short-lived. While bent over, ready to release a good one, without warning, he felt a slap across the back of his head.

"You like that?" Tad laughed.

"Fuck you. That hurt," Mathew responded.

"Well, do something about it. Don't be such a pussy," Tad said, smacking his chest in an attempt to show his dominance.

Mathew did nothing; he knew he could never overpower his cousin.

"What are you gonna do now? Cry? Tell your mama?" Tad said while making a mocking, sad face and putting his fists to his eyes, acting as if he were wiping away tears.

To that day, Mathew did not know where he'd gotten the nerve or the strength to back it up. He waited till Tad was near the edge and then ran at him as fast as he could and pushed Tad over the bypass barrier. As he watched, his cousin fell face-first onto the windshield of a large fuel tanker going under the overpass. The truck skidded out of control, and the back end swung around, passing the front. As the tanker started to tip, Mathew could still see his cousin's body protruding from the glass, still kicking his legs. A small sports car came flying under the overpass and struck the fuel truck just as it landed on its side. The explosion that followed was so powerful that it knocked Mathew to the ground; he could feel the heat of the flames as they tore through the sky. He got up, giggling. It was the greatest day of his life. He dusted off his pants and ran back to the hidden path, hoping no one had seen. Once back under the cover of the woods, Mathew saw his aunt and uncle appear at the back door, looking over the treetops, and within seconds, his father and mother were there as well. The women wore robes, his father was in his boxers, and his uncle was in his pajama bottoms. It was obvious the blast had awakened them, which gave Mathew a ray of hope. He bent down as low as he could get and ran along the path, but just before he got to the backyard, he took the other path leading to the front of the house. With everyone in back, he made his way through the front door, and with his heart pumping a mile a minute, he bolted toward the stairs. Once back in Tad's bedroom, he stripped down to his underwear and lay back in bed. A few minutes later, his mother came up to check on him and Tad but found only Mathew, who was sitting in bed and wiping the sleep from his eyes. They never knew he was with his cousin when it happened. He had gotten away with murder, and it had been easy.

Mathew smiled at the memory, but that day, he was putting that all behind him. This was the last hit. He had pushed it to the limit, but now it was time to let it go. In his ship, he would travel to a place where there were no people—no one he would be forced to tolerate.

A black cat approached him as he made his way down the street. *Please don't cross in front of me*, he thought. He was not normally a suspicious man, but that day, his nerves were on edge. The cat stopped dead in its tracks and looked up at him as he advanced. *What the hell is this? If they cross your path, it's bad luck, and if they don't, it's good luck, but what if the bastard just stops halfway and stares? Is that good luck, worse luck, or what?* The cat did not move as Mathew made a wide circle around it. He thought about giving it a quick kick as he walked by but then thought better of it. As he looked back, the cat was still staring at him, following him with its eyes as he made his way down the street. "Damn," he said aloud. The experience gave him the willies.

While it was early afternoon in Dublin, it was just before dawn in Tampa. Brandy Cartwright awoke to the sound of heavy machinery. She was less than pleased with the commotion outside and rolled out of bed to investigate. It sounded as if the noise were right outside her back door, but as she looked though her front window, she saw that in fact, it was coming from the open lot next to her. Glancing down the street, she saw a truck with an Oversize Load sign pulling a large trailer behind. "Son of a bitch," she said out loud. Someone was moving in right next to her. Of all the open lots, they'd picked the one right up her backside to move into. Around the truck pulled a brand-new pitch-black Cadillac with tinted windows. *The new neighbors*, she thought. Maybe it was not too late; maybe she could talk them into moving farther away. She ran to her bedroom, pulled off her nightgown, and quickly got dressed. Once they met her and found out what a crazy-ass woman she was, maybe they would think twice about living so close. Before she had finished slipping her shirt over her head, she heard a loud knock on the door. *Damn, now what?* she thought.

Brandy made her way through the trailer to the front door. She glanced out and saw the back of a thin woman dressed in a long black dress, and in her driveway was the black Cadillac. Slowly, Brandy opened the door and went straight into her grouchy-old-woman routine. "Can I help you?" she huffed.

"Damn, you're a mean old bitch, aren't you?" the woman replied. She didn't even bother to turn as she said it.

"Now, you look here, lady. I don't know who you think you are, but—"

Before she could finish, the woman turned

around with a large smile on her face. It was her dearest friend in the world, Ethel Johnson. It had been more than forty years, but there was no mistake: it was Ethel, standing right there in the flesh.

On the front step, the two women embraced long and hard. It had been so very long.

"Damn, girl, did you get whiter living up there in that nasty-ass cold weather? Here you are, living in sunny Florida, and you look like a ghost!" Ethel joked.

"Oh, Ethel, it is so great to see you! Come inside," responded Brandy, waving her arms.

"I was going to wait until they had it all set up for me before I came over acting like the new neighbor. I even have Bundt cake in the car to give you, but then they said it could be tomorrow before it's done, and hell, I couldn't wait that long to see you," said Ethel.

"Have a seat at the table, and I'll get us some coffee."

"Man, I bet you were pissed when you saw someone moving right next door with all this open land around here," responded Ethel, picking out a spot at the small, round table.

"More than pissed," Brandy replied. She walked into the kitchen and started the coffeepot.

"Well, I can always find another spot if you

like." Ethel held up both hands. "I mean, if you don't want me here."

"Shut your mouth. You know you are not moving an inch."

"Okay, if you're sure. I mean, there are a lot of other places an old black woman like me can go," Ethel said with a grin.

"All I want to know is how in the hell you found me. The last time I talked to you, I had just moved back to Parksville, and you had just gotten married to Martin. I tried looking you up a bunch of times, but I couldn't find you."

"That's because we moved to Jamaica; then to Canada, of all places; then to New York; and then back to New Orleans. That man kept me on the move. I didn't know if I was coming or going most of the time."

"Did you two get a divorce?" asked Brandy. "I don't mean to be nosy, but here you are, and—"

"No, no, that's okay. That old bastard up and died on me about a year ago. Just when I finally started to like him too."

Brandy returned to the table. "Coffee will be ready in a minute. You still take cream and sugar?"

"Same as always."

As Brandy sat down, Ethel reached across the table and grabbed her by the hand. "God, I missed you," she said, and she started to cry.

"Now, now, what's all this?" asked Brandy.

"I am just so happy to be here. You know, for the first time since you left Louisiana, I feel at home. It was just never right without the two of us being together." Ethel released her hand and pulled a hankie out of the sleeve of her shirt.

Brandy smiled, and she too began to tear up. "Now you're gonna make me cry too, you old cow. Tell me about your life. I've missed so much of it," she said, trying to lighten the mood.

"Not much to tell, actually. When we got married, I kept my family name. Remember, I sang under that name—Madam de Glapion. Anyway, Martin had his band, and I sang in a number of small clubs."

"You never sang for his band?" ask Brandy, surprised.

"Hell no, I didn't even like that shit they played. I stuck to my blues. That's where I came from."

"What about family? You never had any kids?"

"Shit, I forgot you have been gone so long. I had a little girl. I named her Marie. She died at ten—cancer, of all things," Ethel said with a faraway look in her eyes, as if lost in a comforting memory.

"Oh, I am so sorry."

"No, no, no, she was a blessing from God," Ethel said, placing her hand over her heart. "I miss her every day, but while she was here, my life was complete."

"Do you have any pictures of her? I would love to see them."

"Oh, trust me, once that trailer is in place, I will give you a photographic play-by-play of my whole damn life."

Brandy got up to check on the coffee. From the kitchen, she asked, "What about Sonny? How is he doing?"

"My brother died in the war, honey. He was only thirty."

"Oh, I am so sorry to hear that. He was a good man."

"You had the hots for him, didn't you? Now, tell the truth because I'll know," Ethel said with a smirk.

Brandy came back to the table, holding two cups. "Yes, that brother of yours was easy on the eyes and such a great guy," she said. "I think he liked me too."

"Shit, I know he did. You were all that man talked about for the longest time. I know times being what they were made it hard, and I know you was scared for his safety. I mean, if you two had ever hooked up—a black man dating a white woman in Louisiana? He would have ended up dangling at the end of a rope for sure."

Brandy looked Ethel right in the eyes. Even after all those years, Ethel knew her too well.

"Well, what about you? Any other men or any kids on your end?"

"No, after Jack, I just didn't want to get married again. To tell you the truth, I've lived a very boring life, and I've loved every minute of it."

"Well, girl, your life ain't gonna be boring now. Ethel is back in town. You hear me?"

Brandy smiled. The will might have been there, but Brandy knew at their age, they were not going to be setting the world on fire. However, in their day, that had been a different story.

"Do you remember the first time we met? It was at Moe's," Brandy said.

"Oh my God, Moe's. I haven't thought of that place for years. There you were, up onstage with those other girls in those skimpy little outfits, doing that awful cabaret-type dance number."

"Oh please, we had a blast, and the tips were good."

"That's because that bastard Moe made you wait tables in between sets."

"Oh, come on now. Moe gave me my first job after Jack died. If it had not been for him, I might have had to move back to the farm."

"I know. It's just that he was always so grouchy, and he sweat like no one I ever met in my life; he was always dripping wet."

"I remember that first night so clearly. You

got onstage right after we got off, and you started singing 'Stormy Weather.' Oh, girl, could you sing."

"Yeah, that's until that asshole in the front yelled out he wanted to smell my nigger cunt." Ethel paused. "I will never forget how you walked up behind him and poured that whole glass of beer onto his head." Ethel giggled.

"He was out of control. Remember, it was Moe who stood up and ran over when it looked like he was going to take a swing at me. He threw that ass out the door and told him never to come back, remember?"

"We were pretty inseparable after that."

"Well, until you talked me into buying a whorehouse!"

"With my money, sugar," Ethel snapped.

"You just used me 'cause I was white."

"Damn straight. You know they were never going to sell that place to a black woman. They were afraid I would open a black whorehouse."

"Why didn't you, by the way? I mean, why did you drag me into it?" said Brandy sarcastically.

"You knew as well I did that a black whorehouse didn't make no money. With black men and poor whites as customers, we would have gone broke. Drag my ass. Are you kidding me? You acting like you was fighting back or something. You knew what you was doing."

Brandy laughed. "I was an innocent victim."

"Innocent my ass. You took to it like a horse to water, honey, and you never had to pull a single trick yourself."

"Yes, and you got to perform every night for a crowd that was just there for pussy."

"Maybe, but they weren't paying for mine."

The women busted up laughing. It was true; Brandy had run the house, and Ethel had provided the entertainment, but they had shared everything down the middle. They never once had fought over money.

"Damn, we had it good back then," said Ethel. "We were the bells of the ball. I mean, everywhere we went, people bent over and kissed our asses. I don't remember ever buying a drink in any club on Bourbon."

"Hey, I never told you this, but remember that pimp—what was his name?" Brandy thought for a moment. "Henry Holiday?"

"Oh, I remember him all right. That scum ball came into our house and proceeded to tell us that one of our girls belonged to him, and he was going to hurt us bad if we didn't turn her over," Ethel said in her best Pimp Holiday voice.

"That's the one."

"Honey, I paid Theo a hundred bucks to break his nose."

Brandy started laughing so hard she could not catch her breath.

"What the hell is wrong with you?" Ethel said.

It took a few moments for Brandy to regain her composure. Then she replied, "I paid Bubba two to take out his knee!" Again, she started to laugh. "Poor bastard. No wonder we never saw him again." Then they both fell into a fit of laughter.

CHAPTER 3

NEW FRIENDS AND OLD RIVALS

As Phillip rode up to the Burk mansion, he thought it looked unreal, like something out of an old movie. The house was massive, and to the left were large stables that looked empty and forgotten. There was a long white stone drive that ended in a circle around a Roman statue of Neptune. Naked cherubs surrounding the fountain were urinating steady streams of water that cascaded down the gold-plated seashells at Neptune's feet and into a pool below. The house was stone, with gothic windows stretching two stories high in the front of the house on opposite sides of a huge mahogany front door. The house was symmetrical in appearance. There were large, square multipaned windows on the first two floors, but on the third and uppermost floor, there was a vast difference. There the windows were much smaller, farther apart, and understated. At the top of the house, small gargoyle-like figures were nestled into the fabric of the gutters, all facing forward and looking down to the drive below.

Hoffman pulled the car to an abrupt stop in front of the door, and by the time Franky, Shawn, and Phillip had gotten out of the car, he was already banging the door with the brass wolf head knocker.

"Benjamin, it's Timothy!" shouted Hoffman.

There was a long pause, and by the time the trio had gathered around Hoffman on the front step, he was banging again.

"Come on, Ben. I know you can hear me."

"Maybe he isn't here," Shawn said in a soft voice.

"He's here," replied Hoffman. "Why the staff hasn't come to politely get rid of me is the question." Again, he knocked. "Ben, it's important, or I would not be here. You know that."

Slowly, a voice came from behind the door. "Go away, Tim. The answer is still no."

"I have someone here who may change that."

"Doubtful."

"Look and see."

Slowly, the oversize door opened a crack. Phillip saw a pair of eyes peering out past Hoffman and straight at him. "Guest," the voice said softly.

When the door opened, there stood a man dressed only in a fashionable silk robe, holding a snifter of what appeared to be bourbon. "Enter, please," he said, speaking directly to Phillip.

As Phillip walked through the doorway, he was in awe. He had expected some dreary old house with portraits of long-dead relatives hanging on the walls and maybe tapestries, old and musty. Instead, he saw a modern room painted in an eggshell color. The sunlight from the two front windows filled the house with light. There was no furniture other than a reading desk and chair in the main corridor; the space was wide open, with marble tiles for flooring and two staircases, one on each side, in perfect alignment for the windows going up to the second floor.

"In here, please." The man tipped his glass toward the door to the right. "Let's talk in the drawing room, shall we?"

Inside the drawing room were large overstuffed leather recliners, a long sectional coach, and a large ottoman. "Please have a seat," said the host as he plopped down in one of the recliners. As he did so, his night coat parted, exposing a slight peek at his package, and he made no sudden movements to cover it up.

"For God's sake, Ben, no one wants to stare at your oversize pecker!" Hoffman said. "You're drunk."

"We are all men here. Really, Tim, you are a bit uptight, aren't you?" he said in a sarcastic tone. "You are always uptight, and yes, I am fucking drunk. Why do you care?"

"You're such a child!" Hoffman exclaimed.

With that, Benjamin stood up and removed his night coat completely, standing there as naked as the day he was born. He threw the garment over the back of his chair, twisted his body so his penis swung back and forth for a few moments, and then sat back in his chair, slowly reclining with his hands folded behind his head.

"You're an ass," said Hoffman.

"No, I am not an ass. This is an ass," he replied as he stood up, bent over, and stuck his butt in the air.

"Fuck you!" shouted Hoffman, his face red with anger.

Phillip saw Franky making his "Holy shit!" face, and he heard Shawn give a little chuckle. They were both getting a kick out of the scene, especially the reaction from Hoffman.

"Well, I'm ready. How about you?" Benjamin said.

Hoffman did not say another word; he simply turned and stormed out of the room. They heard the front door slam shut behind him.

Phillip did not know what to do. Should they follow? Should they apologize for being there?

Benjamin looked at him for a moment, and a huge smile came over his face. "Sorry. He gets me going. I'm Benjamin Burk. You can call me Ben if you like; my best friends do," he said as he rerobed. "I am so sorry to put you through all this, especially since you have traveled all the way from the States."

"How did you know?" asked Franky, but Benjamin continued.

"You are Mr. Phillip Parker," he said, and he reached out his hand. Phillip was reluctant at first but then took it. "Pleased to meet you."

"Thank you. Pleased to meet you as well."

Benjamin then walked over to Franky. "And this is Franky Lake. I loved your paper on Milton's perception of binary opposition, by the way," he said, shaking his hand.

"Well, thanks," responded Franky. He was obviously taken aback. Few had read that work, and he'd almost forgotten about it himself.

"I am sorry, but I do not know your name," he said as he reached for Shawn's hand.

"My name is Shawn Davis," he replied.

"Shawn Davis the cameraman? You did the Winchester house with Tim a few years back. Is that correct?"

"How did you know that?" Shawn said.

"Maybe next time you will look to see who is signing your paycheck. I funded that little expedition. But please, everyone, sit down, and tell me why you are here."

"You know why we are here," said Phillip, playing a little of Benjamin's own game.

"I do," he replied, impressed.

"I saw the salt line below the front door as we came in, and there is another one over there below that window." Phillip looked over at the front window. "You know what we are here for, but first, I would like to ask something."

Shawn looked a little shocked at his firmness; Franky, however, had been waiting for this since the moment they'd walked through the door. Phillip had always been one to get to the point, and in certain situations, he did not care if he pissed others off in doing it.

"How is it you know so much about Banthom?" asked Phillip. He sat up, leaning in, obviously knowing that question would answer a number of other questions down the line. Shawn's and Franky's faces showed looks of anticipation.

"Did you know that this house has beneath it a trove of historical artifacts dating back to the thirteenth century, all housed in an actual dungeon that was here long before this house was built?" He had everyone's undaunted attention at that point. "This house was built over the ruins of a castle, possibly the summer castle of Dublin Castle, built in 1204 by King John of England himself. If so, this castle was owned and occupied not by a king but by the church. The dungeon and its artifacts have been in the Burk family since the time of Henry VIII of England. In that dungeon were found two of the three Grand Grimoires known to exist."

"A large black book written in Latin—backward Latin, to be precise?" Phillip said.

"Yes, Phillip, the very one you took from the church," responded Benjamin.

"Okay, I am lost," Shawn said. He had been quiet long enough. "Phillip, you're talking about salt in the windows and ancient books. I'm sorry, but someone needs to catch me up here."

"A grimoire is a book of spells," answered Benjamin. "The Grand Grimoires are books containing the most powerful spells and potions learned through the ages and throughout the world—spells of Egyptian priests and druids, gypsy curses, Babylonian and Sumerian hexes, satanic and coven's rituals throughout Europe all captured in one book. You see, witches have limited power unto themselves, but with the Grand Grimoires, they can manipulate evil forces around them to do their bidding, and that's what these books do. They tell you the words and potions needed to manipulate these forces. With that kind of power, a witch could become unstoppable."

"So what happened to the books? Obviously, Banthom and Fritz each had a copy," asked Phillip.

"When my family found out what they might be, they contacted a priest, who in turn contacted the Vatican. It was ordained that the Burks would have one family member at all times be a member of the church—a priest or nun who would guard the books against evil forces that may desire them for themselves. Their secrecy was the key, you see. In the early seventeenth century, the house was robbed, and with all the treasures housed in the dungeon, only the books were taken. One of my ancestors, Father Marcus Burk, was killed while trying to protect the books. That's him on the wall behind me."

All the men looked up at the portrait of a man dressed in black robes and holding a Bible in his right hand. Phillip thought his face was strong and dignified.

"That is when the church sent for Father McDonald to come to Dublin."

Franky and Phillip looked at each other in shock.

"Yes, Phillip, the same Father McDonald who left the journal," said Benjamin.

"He was sent here to recover the books!" said Phillip. "That's why he came, but in his journal—"

"I know what he wrote in his journal. I have the complete copy upstairs in my bedroom closet. You see, he kept two: one for the priest of the church in Michigan and one for the keepers of the books, the

Burk family. Their responsibilities for the book had not diminished because they sent for a priest. If anything, they became more demanding. You see, it was their responsibility to keep the books safe. The journal you are in possession of is limited in detail. Am I correct?"

"Yes, almost half a story," replied Franky.

"That's because no one other than a Burk or the pope needs to know the powers they contain, should someone else find one of the books first. McDonald wrote about your Parksville and building a church in what is now called Jackson. That is how I know about you and Franky. Like you, I followed the local press. I had a copy of your Sunday Jackson paper mailed to me every week. When the deaths started coming to Parksville, I followed. By the time I arrived in your quaint village, the whole ordeal was over. I know Fritz, our Fritz, died in that house fire. I also know you two," he said, pointing to Franky and then Phillip, "were involved in the whole affair. I did my digging, and with my funds, I can dig pretty damn deep. I knew Fritz's copy of the book and McDonald's journal were stolen from the church, and I knew it had to be one of you who did it. The feds were watching you closely, but you covered your tracks well."

"You were watching us?" Franky said. He shuddered at the thought of being followed.

"Please. I even sat in on one of Phillip's lectures. I asked a few questions, as I recall," he said with a smirk. "You have to remember I was younger then, not much older than Franky at the time. I fit in nicely."

"Why didn't you confront us and tell us of this then?" asked Phillip.

"To tell you the truth, I had hoped that was the end of this for you. I'd seen how much he had taken away from you both. Upon my return to Dublin, I purchased Banthom House—paid twice what it was worth. As for Banthom's book, it was still here in this very house. You see, he was captured here in Dublin and brought to this house along with his book. In the middle of the night, he was dragged off by the families of those he had converted. The Burks never really knew his fate. What I did with the book I cannot tell, but it's safe."

"Does Hoffman know all this?" Shawn asked. Everyone had almost forgotten he was even there, as he had listened so quietly.

"I told him of my family history and about Banthom. He didn't believe me, even about my trip to the States and the two of you. He thought I'd made it up to keep him from doing his investigation of the house. There is no doubt you two are being used as the catalyst to get him access to the house. How did he contact you?"

"Believe it or not, we contacted him," responded

Phillip with a grin. "That explains his lack of questions."

"Interesting. So he knew you were coming and put together a team of investigators," he said, looking over at Shawn, "thinking I would say yes if you were here."

"No, I think we were a bonus. I know he said he would not have gotten the chance to do the investigation if it had not been for Ms. Bradley," Phillip responded.

"Josette Bradley?" Benjamin asked. He did not wait for a response. "How in the hell did he get her to agree to this?"

"Yes, Ms. Josette Bradley."

"She is one of the most sought-out mediums in the world. I met her once in London just after a missing-child case she helped the Yard solve. No one knew she had anything to do with the apprehension of the perpetrator, but she did. She told the police right where to find the body—and the bodies of thirteen other missing children. You see, I have connections with the Yard as well as the Garda Síochána," he said with a look of pride. "I was in Piccadilly for a fund-raiser. Can't remember which one—for starving children around the world, I think. I go to so many it is hard to keep them straight. She donated a large sum, as I remember. If not for my friends at the Yard, I would never have even known who she was. Frail little thing. It seems these investigations took a lot out of her. I heard she refused to do any more under any circumstances, and now here she is. How very strange. Don't you think?"

"I really could not say," replied Phillip.

"So with the murders, Tim saw his chance?" Benjamin said with a look of bewilderment. "But how did Tim convince her? It couldn't have been with money—he doesn't have any."

"Maybe we could just ask him," Shawn said. "Do you want me to go see if he will come back in?"

"No, no, I think that is something I must do," said Benjamin as he got up out of his chair.

After Professors Hoffman, Lake, and Parker had left with the cameraman Shawn for their appointment with Mr. Burk, Joe, Mary, and Josette were left alone to comprehend everything they had just been told. Looking back on now, Josette wished she could have been more convincing to Mary that the investigation could be dangerous. "We may encounter something at this location we wish we had not," Josette had said. "Evil does not simply go away; sometimes traces can linger forever if not dealt with properly."

Joe had taken no convincing at all. He'd made it clear after the foursome left that he was done with the whole thing. He'd pulled no bones about the small wages Dr. Hoffman was offering and said the money was not worth the idea of investigating the home of a known devil worshipper. Mary, on the other hand, had not seemed to believe a word of it. Josette once again had tried to emphasize that what Hoffman had said was true. "This man was known for multiple murders. It is said he was into eating human flesh. That is the darkest kind of spirit there is."

Mary had been unmoved. "Really, I don't care about any of that. The whole thing is ridiculous. I am not giving up this sweet gig because of some fairy tale. Even if this guy was a witch or whatever, that was over two hundred years ago. Who cares now?"

As Joe and Josette had gotten ready to leave Hoffman's apartment, Josette had looked back and seen Mary cleaning up the day's mess. "You sure you don't need a hand with this?" she had asked, feeling bad about leaving when there was work to be done.

"I'm fine. Trust me. It's not the first time I've cleaned up after one of his get-togethers," Mary had responded with a wave of her hand. "Go get some sleep."

Thinking about it now as she walked the four blocks to her hotel, Josette doubted Mary had been telling the whole truth. She did not see Hoffman having many, if any, get-togethers. Oh, to be that young again and so full of energy. She could feel the girl's desire for life. She also picked up on a couple of her other desires as well, such as her fascination with Franky and Shawn. She would have liked to attribute that to her psychic abilities, but one did not need to be a psychic to see what vibes Mary was putting out.

The day was cool, and the city streets were full of sounds and motion. Somehow, that comforted her; she had thought twice about Joe's offer for a ride but finally decided against it. She did not have a good feeling about him, and she had learned over the years to trust her feelings. It was not a feeling that he would try to take advantage of her or anything like that but, rather, a feeling that he had a date with darkness—and it was coming soon. Somehow, he would be involved in something that would cause a great deal of pain. She had seen the darkness like a shadow over his head. Sometimes she got strong feelings, and nothing happened, but many times, her premonitions came true. *Better safe than sorry*, she thought.

Josette deliberated the strange chain of events that had brought her there to that day in her life. She had always had the gift. For as long as she could remember, it had been there. Little did her mom know, when she'd been young and played with imaginary friends, they had not been figments of her imagination but spirits of those who had passed. Her aunt Mae knew, and from the time she was little, Aunt Mae had been the only one she could talk with about her strange dreams, the visits from the dead, and her ability to foresee things yet to happen. Aunt Mae had called her abilities "the gift." Aunt Mae said that was what her grandmother had called it when she found out Aunt Mae had it. In fact, to Josette, it was a gift she could have lived without, because many times, the gift turned into a nightmare. Aunt Mae had warned Josette to keep it a secret, as people knowing would cause her a life of pain.

No one in her family other than her aunt had any idea of her abilities, and she intended to keep it that way, even after she solved her first case. Josette was only twenty when she moved alone to London. Within a week, she had gotten a job at an upper-crust restaurant just outside Piccadilly Circus, signed a lease for a lovely one-bedroom flat not far from work, and started dating a man she had met at the local pub. Life was good—until spirits started coming to her for help. The first was the ghost of Maggie O'Malley, a sixteen-year-old girl from Liverpool who visited her every night for a month in her dreams. She knew at once who Maggie was because her face had been on the box every day for the past two weeks. She'd gone missing while walking home from school. Maggie's spirit never said a word but would show itself at the foot of her bed, dressed in a tattered, bloodstained dress. She would point out her window to her neighbor Robert Winston's home across the street. Every night, it was the same: not a word, just her bony little finger pointing. Finally, Josette could not take the visits any longer and called in an anonymous tip to Scotland Yard. It seemed that kind old Mr. Winston had a thing for young girls. In his hall closet, they found Maggie's body. The police believed she had been raped and tortured to death. They believed she had been dead for a month and a half, but he was still using her to satisfy his perverted needs. Once the ordeal was over, Maggie did not visit anymore, but others came—usually children but some adults as well. Over the next five years, she gave her tips, and over those five years, six men and one woman were sent off to prison. Maggie had been a day at the beach compared to those who came after, because their murders were not just next door, and they took investigation.

Going to sights seen in her dreams, she would often have to relive every minute of pain and suffering through the eyes of the victim. It was a catch twenty-two because the spirits would not leave her alone if she did nothing, but for them to move on, she had to suffer. Inspector Stills finally showed up one day at her door. He had done the work of solving many murders with her tips and knew there had to be something extra special about the lady who refused to leave her name. She agreed to cooperate with Scotland Yard as long as her name was never mentioned. Stills agreed since working with a psychic would not have made good press for the Yard. Then she had even more deaths to deal with—more untimely murders, more children, and more beaten women. It got to be too much. After two years, she confided in Stills that she could not keep reliving the deaths of so many; it was taking too much out of her. She would have to quit. There was no argument from Stills; he confided in her that he had been expecting it for some time. How she had done it that long was beyond him.

Going forward, Josette came to realize that if she did not use her gift, then her gift would use her. She started giving private readings and performing psychic investigations. The investigations were often for nothing, but sometimes she was able to help lost spirits move on. She soon had a reputation for cleaning houses, for which, she found out, people were willing to pay huge amounts of money. As she used her gift, the spirits of those tortured souls stopped seeking her out, and for the first time in her life, her gift was just that—a gift. To that day, her family had no idea how she earned a living.

The smell of fresh-baked goods wafted in the

air, and up the street she saw a bakery. Maybe she'd have a little something; it was nearing noon.

Hoffman had been watching through the drawing room window as the men talked. The moment he'd stepped outside the door, a feeling of melancholy had come over him. He knew what a fool he had been. He had deserved everything Benjamin had given him. The flashing of his naked body had been a little over the top, but maybe he'd deserved that too—a prick for a prick. More importantly, he feared he might be blowing his last shot to get Benjamin to submit. Through the years, Benjamin had been nothing but kind to him and had funded many of his expeditions, but his own desire to prove there was something after life was so strong that it had cost him his job at Harvard, every female relationship he'd ever had, and every friend he'd ever made. He knew that when he had gone to Benjamin about Banthom House, it had not been easy for Benjamin to tell him about his family's belief in witches, their role as the great keepers of mystic books, and their duty of keeping humankind out of the hands of evil. Benjamin had warned him that Banthom was an evil spirit that must be left to lie in peace undisturbed, least he arise and doom them all to a hell on earth. Even though he personally thought it was foolish, he knew Benjamin believed it all. How insane it was that the man who made it possible for him to pursue his life's ambition was the same man who denied him his golden fleece. The moment Phillip had said his name on the phone, Hoffman had known he had taken a giant leap toward fulfilling his quest.

Hoffman felt something on his pant leg; he looked down to see a black cat rubbing against him. "Well, little fella, where did you come from?" he said, reaching down to give it a scratch.

He had been obsessed with that damn house since he had moved to Dublin. He knew if he was ever going to prove the existence of a life force after death, he would do it at Banthom House. Now, because of his own anger, he might have walked out on his only chance.

The cat made a smooth purring sound and rubbed its face against Hoffman's shin. He reached down again; picked it up; found a chair in the front garden, his favorite spot; and sat down with the cat in his lap.

"Tim?" called Benjamin from the front door. "Are you still out there?"

Slowly, Hoffman rose to his feet. It was time to face whatever was coming his way. "I'm coming," he said, and he slowly made his way toward Benjamin's voice.

As they greeted each other at the door, Hoffman

remembered he was still carrying the cat. He set the cat down and reached out his hand. "I am so truly sorry for the way I've behaved," he said, not looking up at Benjamin.

"Water under the bridge," Benjamin replied half-heartedly. Hoffman raised his head and met Benjamin's unforgiving eyes.

As they were speaking, the cat sauntered through the open front door. Neither man realized what was going on. They were both focused on finding words to break the awkward silence that followed.

Mary Todd received the call from Dr. Hoffman at about five o'clock that the meeting had gone well and that they were on their way back. He told her to go ahead leave for the day and return the next morning, as they would be gathering at his place to finalize the plans to investigate the house. Mary told him about Joe's change of heart regarding the investigation, but he did not seem the least bit upset. "I will call and talk to him," he said. "We have decided the investigation will be in the light of day. It's unusual but necessary."

When Mary hung up, she was disappointed she would not see Franky before she left. She'd been hoping to ask him out to dinner and maybe back to her place for a little dessert. She knew now that he was the one she wanted. There was something about him—the way he carried himself. He was proud and self-assured. Shawn was cute, but Franky was more mature and mysterious.

Once she was back in her modest flat, her only thoughts were of taking a hot shower, grabbing a quick bite, and relaxing. Besides working for Hoffman and being a full-time student, Mary spent time volunteering with many different charities, including the Assisi Animal Sanctuary Charity and the Dublin Historical Society. It was just as well she had not hooked up that night; she was beat. She had spent most of the day trying to decipher Hoffman's lecture notes that he wanted typed and filed. Like everything else about the man, his filing was disorganized and confusing, but she had muddled through.

She walked into the bathroom, turned on the shower, and slowly undressed in front of the mirror of the medicine cabinet. Mary was proud of her body; she had what she considered to be perfect breasts, not too large but not too small. As she looked at them, she arched her back, admiring how firm and straight they were. Her pink nipples were protruding outward. She began to rub them with her open palm, and the feeling sent a shock wave through her body. She could imagine Franky behind her, fondling them from behind. She imagined his large, warm hands gliding slowly over her entire body, making their way southward farther and farther and brushing against her small patch of perfectly shaped hair. His other hand would grope her firm ass. "Screw it," she said aloud. "The shower can wait." She turned it off and returned to her bedroom.

On the drive back to Dr. Hoffman's, all was quiet. Phillip figured everyone must be deep in thought after all that had transpired. Dr. Hoffman had gotten his way. They could investigate the house; Benjamin had been clear about that. However, Phillip had insisted it happen during the day. He knew from experience that half-human monsters didn't tend to stroll around in broad daylight. If Banthom was in the house, he would be hiding. They would need to look for some sign of the two kids digging somewhere around the house. There was no doubt the kids found in Parksville Cemetery in Michigan had dug up the creature that would kill them. Somehow, like Kip before them, they'd heard his pleas to set him free. There was no reason to believe anything had been different in Dublin. If they found an empty grave, then there was no doubt Banthom had indeed come back.

"So this Banthom creature—do you think he will show himself?" asked Shawn sheepishly.

"Who can say?" responded Franky before

Phillip could say a word. "I know I am taking no chances. I will be packing flammables and a box of matches."

"You lost me again," said Shawn with a confused look on his face.

"The bastard needs to burn, or it doesn't die. It just keeps coming back," responded Franky.

Phillip was going to add to the comment but changed his mind. Franky had said all there was to say.

"Well, if he has been killing all these people, how come we have not heard anything on the news? I mean, if he has been leaving bodies all over the place, then why haven't we heard about it?" Shawn said.

"That is a good question," Dr. Hoffman said.

Phillip simply responded, "I don't know."

"You don't believe in all this, do you, Dr. Hoffman?" asked Shawn.

"Sorry, but no, not really. I do believe there is an evil spirit in that house, but I do not believe he is flesh and blood." He looked over at Phillip and offered his apologies. "Sorry."

"That's all right. You will believe before it's all over," Phillip replied, and he turned to stare out the window into the twilight sky.

"I think he's smarter than your witch," said Shawn, speaking half to himself. "He's taking his time and hiding what he kills. Maybe we need to ask Benjamin to use his connections to see if there are any missing persons in town. You said he was their leader. Maybe he was their leader for a reason." With that, no more was said.

Phillip had underestimated that young man. He was on to something important. Banthom and Fritz were different. Maybe Banthom was smarter, taking his time to learn the world around him a little more. He feared this expedition might be more than he and Franky had bargained for.

Upon returning to their car, Franky and Phillip offered their goodbyes. They had agreed to meet again in the morning, this time with Benjamin, to go over everything he knew about the manuscript, the books, and his family's history with Banthom. They agreed to drop Shawn off at his hotel and headed to their own. Both exhausted, they agreed to order room service and turn in. Tomorrow was going to be a long day.

Benjamin Burk did not see the cat until he was ready for bed. He had walked back into the room they had met in just a few hours before to turn off the lights, and there it was, asleep under the chair where Hoffman had been sitting. "I'll be damned! How did you get in here?" he asked. "You must have snuck in when the door was open." Slowly, he picked it up and walked toward the front door.

The cat seemed almost lethargic, as if it could not care less that it was being put out. "Now, you go home, wherever that is," Benjamin said, opening the door and setting the cat down on the stoop. The cat arched, stretched, and then simply ambled away into the moonlight. Benjamin never noticed its tail was coated with white salt crystals.

He shut the door and made his way across the room to the staircase. He thought about Phillip and how much he liked the man. He'd hate to tell him he'd had staff break into his house a number of times to recover the book. Maybe he would keep that part to himself. After all, he was sure the man must be trying to make up his mind about his intentions, and that information surely would not help.

As he ascended, he had a nagging feeling he was not alone. He tried to pass it off as his imagination, but it persisted as he climbed, until he had to react. He quickly turned and looked behind him down the steps, but there was nothing to see. Maybe he just had the jitters; he'd had a long day after all. As he turned to go up the stairs once again, he heard the strangest sound, like the call of a sick animal, coming from downstairs. Once again, he turned only to see nothing behind him. "Shit!" he said aloud. "Is someone there?" He heard not a sound. He stood on the steps for a good five minutes, just staring into the darkness at the bottom of the stairs. He started to turn once more, when suddenly, from the kitchen, there came a scurrying sound, as if some large beast were running on all fours on the kitchen tile.

"I said is anyone there?" he yelled. "Tim? Phillip?"

There was no reply. Quiet as a mouse, he moved down the stairs. It took what seemed an eternity to reach the bottom step. His eyes kept darting back and forth as he descended. He stopped and heard nothing. Slowly, he moved toward the kitchen, purposely avoiding the door beneath the stairs. On the way, he grabbed a crystal candlestick off a small table in the hall. As the kitchen light illuminated the room, he realized there was nothing for him to see. Everything looked in order; there was nothing out of place. As he made his way toward the stove to see the entire room, he stopped. A thought abruptly struck him: Why was he holding a candlestick, when he had a gun? He needed his fucking gun. It was upstairs by his nightstand. If there was something in his house, it was not friendly—of that he was sure. Slowly, he backed out, leaving the light on. Once again, he made his way down the hall, and once again, he avoided the door under the stairs. As his hand reached out for the banister for his turn up the stairs, he heard more scurrying, this time from the drawing room next to him. Chills ran the length of his body. Then came the stench. Benjamin could not recall ever smelling something so rancid. He made up his mind right then: he would make a quick dash to his room to get his gun. Unfortunately, he did not make it past the third step.

Chapter 4

ALONE IN THE DARK

A bright red-and-green neon light shone through the window of her hotel room. Josette, who was just settling in for the night, thought about closing the thick greenish curtains but then changed her mind. She felt comforted by the light. Somehow, it made her feel safer.

What a day it had been. She had met some truly pleasant people that morning, and she was glad to be out in the world once again. Though the thought terrified her, she was eager to be on another case. Investigations always took a toll on her, she knew, but solving a crime and taking evil beings off the streets almost made it all worthwhile. She knew she had pressed herself too hard before, wanting to save the world from sociopaths and murderers. This time, she would take it slowly and pace herself.

She had made up her mind that in the morning,

she would confide in the group the reason she was so willing to take on that investigation. It was because of the pleading spirit, which was not an ordinary ghost but a spirit guide. Guides often needed a good reason to punch a hole from their world to the physical world. Unlike earthbound spirits, they were sometimes shrouded with a heavenly glow, as was the case this time. The guide had visited her relentlessly for months; it was always polite but also determined. It would speak endlessly about an evil presence that threatened to take away those the spirit had cared about, and it had told her all about the goings-on in Dublin. It had told her she would be approached by Dr. Hoffman, and it had even told her that without her help, bad things would happen to a lot of good, innocent people. Lastly, it had told her something she had not expected—something about herself and what the investigation could mean for her future. The apparition came every night at midnight, as precise as clockwork. Looking at the clock, she knew she would be getting a visit soon. Josette didn't know a lot about the spirit, even if it was male or female, for it hid in the light, and the voice was unrecognizable. She knew that when it was ready, it would show itself and, if asked, reveal its true name. Unlike unholy spirits, who hid their identities lest they be cast out, guides held to the truth of who they were, once they were ready to do so.

Josette put on her nightgown and climbed into bed. She took a book from the nightstand and started to read. She would know when it arrived.

Lord Benjamin Burk slowly opened his eyes; the bump on the back of his head was sending an ache throughout his entire body. In the dim light coming from under the door at the top of the stairs, he saw steel bars circling his entire head. He knew at once what it was: the head cage. The medieval device was in his collection and was kept in the dungeon. Panic overtook him as he realized where he was. His anxiety multiplied when he felt something moving in the cage with him.

"Book!" said a disembodied voice far behind him.

As he turned his head to see who had spoken, he came face-to-face with an enormous rat looking for its way out. Burk screamed and tried to flail his arms and legs to no avail; they were strapped tightly with rope to support beams on either side of him.

"Book!" said the unnerving voice once more, this time from his right.

As he jerked his body, he heard the rat hissing at him to stop.

"Book!" screamed the hidden figure.

"What book? I don't know what you are talking about. I have thousands of books," Benjamin said, trying his best to play the part of ignorance.

"Grimoires," the figure replied, this time from the front. The creature in the dark was obviously circling him.

"Who are you?" asked Benjamin, already knowing the answer.

"Banthom." It pronounced the name as if the very mention should strike fear into Benjamin's heart.

"Banthom was killed centuries ago."

A vile laugh came blasting from behind Benjamin's left ear. The sound again angered the rat, which scurried to the other side of the cage and stopped just under Benjamin's nose. In a panic, Benjamin blew on the rat to make it move. It squeaked but stayed where it was, not moving until it was ready. To Benjamin, it seemed like an eternity.

"Why are you here? I have no grimoires. I don't even know what that is. Please, take whatever you want and go."

There was a long pause. Then, from the other side of the room, the voice said, "No mercy here."

To Benjamin, it seemed the words were not directed toward him but sounded more like a memory. He knew Banthom had been tortured there by the Burks as well as the townspeople who had lost their kin. Maybe they had put that very cage on his head in an effort to get him to talk before dragging him off in the middle of the night, never to be heard from again.

"Banthom died two hundred years ago. I had nothing to do with that or you."

Benjamin felt Banthom's breath as he blew gently on the back of his neck and said, "Hunger."

That, he knew, was directed to him. Benjamin thought about the creature's need to feed, but he also knew his desire for the book. "I know nothing. Do you hear me, you bastard? Nothing."

With that, Benjamin felt a scrape along his cheek. The thing had stuck a finger through the cage and cut him with one of its long dark nails, and he could feel blood dripping down his face. "Rat, feed." Another nail glided over but did not cut his midsection. "I feed."

Benjamin understood his meaning all too well. If he waited too long to tell him where the book was, the starving rat would eventually be drawn by the smell of blood from his cheek and begin to eat. Then, if no answer was given, the creature too would feed. "Fuck you!" was all he said. To his amazement, there was no reply. He heard the door leading to the kitchen open, and light poured in for a moment. Then Banthom and the light were gone. The creature was searching the house, gone for now, leaving him alone in the darkness—well, not totally alone.

It was a quarter past midnight when Phillip got the call from a distressed Josette. On his way over to her hotel with Franky in tow, he debated the reason for her call. "All I know is she said it was urgent and that we had to meet her out in front of her hotel," said Phillip.

"And she gave no reason?" Franky said.

"I told you. She just said that it may be a matter of life and death and to please hurry."

"Do you think she called anyone else?"

"I don't know; she didn't say."

"Do you think she really can, you know, talk to the dead?"

"We did."

"Yes, but that was in our dreams. We didn't really see them outside of the dreams."

It hit Phillip like a ton of bricks: in all that had happened in Parksville, he never once had confided in the boy that he had seen spirits come back for their lost souls. At the lake, as the witch Fritz burned, all the dead had come back one by one to claim what they had lost. He'd forgotten that Franky had struck a tree and been knocked out for a short period when it happened.

"I believe she can. For some reason, I trust in

her completely," Phillip said, deciding to wait for another day to convey the events of that night long ago.

"There is a certain innocence about her."

"I think she will be the one to guide us."

"I thought that's why we were funding Hoffman—to guide us," said Franky sarcastically.

"I don't know about him," responded Phillip.

"I think he's an asshole, to tell you the truth."

"And so does Benjamin, obviously."

"No kidding. Can you believe that? I didn't know what the fuck to say when that all went down. Man, those two do not get along."

"Something tells me there is more to it than we will ever know. I know that Benjamin does not trust him, not one bit."

As they turned the last corner, there she was, standing on the sidewalk in front of her hotel. She saw them at once and started waving her arms to let them know she was there. She had on a knitted jacket much too thin for the brisk night air. On her face was a look of urgency.

Mathew Duryee lurked in the shadows outside the Gate Theatre. In a few moments, the crowds would begin to pour out into the night air. For the first time in years, he thought about having a cigarette. Funny, he had not thought about it in so long. Cigarettes left traces, and in his field of work, one could not leave traces, which was why he'd given them up. Still, somehow, that night, he knew if he'd had one, he would have smoked it.

Once he spotted his target, he would work his way through the crowd, cause a distraction, walk up behind him, slit his throat, and then vanish in the sea of hysterical onlookers. This job was the one that would put him on Easy Street for the rest of his life, a ten-million-dollar hit. They said the man he was sent to kill was untouchable—but not for Mathew. He was the best in his chosen profession. His informant had said that his mark had tickets to see a play that night, some Shakespearian bullshit no doubt. He hated the theater, and mostly, he hated people who went to the theater and acted as if they enjoyed it. The source also had said the target had two bodyguards. If need be, Mathew would take them out as well. He was not getting paid for additional kills, so he hoped the distraction was a good one. He would try to spot someone elderly or pregnant or even a child he could trip or push down close to the target, someone needing help, and then the hit would happen in a heartbeat. After one swift stroke of his blade, before anyone knew what had happened, down the road he would walk without any indication of urgency. His heart started to beat faster in anticipation, and droplets of sweat beaded on his oversize forehead. He loved the feeling of excitement and the adrenaline rush he felt just before a kill. Sometimes after a kill, he would find himself fully erect. It was euphoric, a high. It was what made his life worth living. He never killed for pleasure anymore, only for money, but he still got pleasure from it every time he did.

As the crowd let out, Mathew knew at once something was wrong. His target was not there, but the police were, appearing from the theater, the pub across the street, and cars along the drive. He knew he was made. Thinking quickly, he walked briskly across the street, but he did not escape the eyes of his pursuers. As he looked over his shoulder, he saw them reaching for their guns. He had been set up; someone had tipped them off. Not knowing what else to do, he started to run. That was when he heard the first shot ring out. He heard a scream come from the crowd as the people scattered. Another shot sounded. This one hit a tree just in front of him, leaving a large indent in the bark. A Mercedes slammed on its brakes right in front of him. If he'd gone a few more feet, he would have been done running for good. Mathew ran to the driver's-side door, opened it, and threw the elderly lady driving the car forcibly onto the street. He jumped in but not before another shot tore through his right shoulder. Speeding away, he could hear shots hitting the car; one busted out the back window. He'd gotten away, but looking down at the blood seeping from his body, he knew he wouldn't make it far without help.

Immediately, flashing lights were on his back bumper. Flying down Parnell Square, Mathew jumped the curb and made the sharp turn onto O'Connell, and as he did, pain shot through his shoulder, reaching the back of his neck. This was it. This was how he was going to die. Up ahead, a large truck was stopped in the middle of the street. Mathew jumped onto the large walking median that ran down the middle of O'Connell as pedestrians jumped out of his way. Passing the truck, he pulled back into the street once more. The maneuver seemed to buy him a little time, as the sirens and lights seemed somewhat more distant. At the O'Connell monument, Mathew took a sharp left onto Eden Quay and then another onto Marlborough, going the wrong way against traffic. Thank God the street was empty. Quickly, he made another left into the alley of Harbour Court, where he stopped, shut off the car, and waited. Mathew knew that eventually, if he stayed on the road, they would have him for sure; hiding was his only chance. No sooner had he stopped than he heard sirens flying down Eden Quay, just a block away. Though he heard many of the sirens dashing straight down Eden Quay, he heard one turn onto Marlborough. *This may be it*, he thought. Mathew slouched down in his seat, wondering if he had gone up the alley far enough. Could they see the back window? It was a dead giveaway. Should he run? The flashing lights were now making their way up the street. All they needed to do was slow down enough and look up the alley past the trash bins, and it would be all over.

In the darkness, Benjamin could feel the rat's every move. He tried to keep his head tilted to the side the blood was dripping from to keep it from getting a taste, because once it did, there would be nothing he could do about it. Benjamin knew two things for certain: Banthom would never find the book in his house, and he would be back with more questions. He would never give up trying to find the Grand Grimoires, the books with all the knowledge he would ever need. Then another thought came to him: if the rat did not do the trick, there were other torture devices in the dungeon that might: the boot, thumbscrew, Spanish donkey, pear of anguish, Judas cradle, and heretic's fork. The collection was impressive, and Benjamin knew the dungeon held them all. He wondered which, if any, of those devices they had used on Banthom and if Banthom would in turn use them on him. The thought sent shivers down his spine. Benjamin also knew that regardless of whether he told Banthom the location of the book or not, he was a dead man. It was just a matter of time. He had tried to free himself from his binds, but it was not to be. The ropes simply dug deeper into his wrists, adding to the pain. He ached. He wanted to sit down, lower his arms, and end the pain surging through his body. "Lord, please take me," he said into the open air.

"Your lord has no power here," said a voice from behind. Banthom was back. The waiting was over; whatever was going to happen was going to happen. Maybe he would end it quickly. Maybe if Benjamin angered him enough, he would strike out, and that would be that.

"You are the son of a whore," Benjamin blurted out.

"Yes, I am," Banthom replied.

"You will burn in hell," Benjamin responded. He knew in his heart that nothing would ever shake the foul creature.

"That I will," the witch replied. Then Benjamin felt the tie of his robe slowly undone, and in the darkness, he sensed the creature kneel before him. He felt his breath on his bare stomach; that was it, he thought. With one good bite, it would be all over.

"Feed?" asked Banthom. "Or information?"

"Go fuck yourself."

"More fun then," Banthom said in his slow, methodical tone.

Benjamin's only thoughts went to the collection of torture devices.

Just then, the door at the top of the steps flew open, and light came bursting through.

"Benjamin, you down there?" said the voice of Phillip Parker.

Benjamin heard a loud hiss and then the sound of the creature as he scurried out of view.

"Phillip, watch out! He is down here!"

Just then, the lights came on in the dungeon. Phillip had flipped the switch at the top of the stairs. Benjamin's eyes stung, and the rat jumped.

"Is he still there?" This time, it was the voice of Franky.

"I don't see him. Be careful!" Benjamin said.

At the bottom of the stairs, Phillip saw Benjamin's perilous circumstances. His first impulse was to run over and give aid, but he knew better. His eyes searched all the open spaces of the dungeon.

"Is there any other way out of here?" asked Phillip.

"No. Now, please hurry."

The other two slowly made their way down the stairs, and just as Franky reached the bottom step, he was sent flying through the air and crashed into the wooden shelving near the entrance. None of them knew exactly what had taken place. They did not see Banthom make his escape, but the door at the top of the steps slammed shut.

The rat, startled by all the commotion, attacked, biting Benjamin repeatedly on the back of the head and his left ear.

Benjamin screamed.

Phillip ran over and flung open the latch to the cage. Without any hesitation, he reached in, grabbed the rat by its tail, and flung it across the floor. It slid all the way to the steps, just in front of Josette, who was helping Franky to his feet. She seemed to give no notice.

"I'm all right," Franky told her as he stood, holding his head. "Let me help Phillip."

As Phillip and Franky worked eagerly to free Benjamin, Josette kept her eyes peeled to make sure the creature was not coming back. Once freed, Benjamin slumped to the floor. It took a few minutes for the men to figure out how to release the cage from his head, but once they pulled the pin, it came crashing to the floor, where Benjamin gave it a swift kick.

Josette at once ran over to examine the bites. "He is bleeding pretty badly. We need to get him to the hospital as soon as possible."

"Yes, let's not wait," responded Phillip. Then he turned to Franky. "You need to be checked as well. You hit hard—I heard it."

"I'm fine," replied Franky. "Let's just get the fuck out of here. For all we know, the son of a bitch is upstairs waiting for us."

With that, the men lifted Benjamin off the floor and half carried him up the steps.

Chapter 5

A MEETING OF MINDS

Shawn awoke to the sun shining through his hotel room window. He hated waking up alone, especially in a hotel room far from home, but he knew he needed that job. Three months to the day after losing Samantha, the love of his life, he'd received the call from Hoffman. Shawn had sworn he would never work with the man again after the Winchester house, but any project was good for him now—anything that would take his mind off the pain. Sam had been his other half and made him complete, and with her gone, life just didn't seem to be important anymore. There was an emptiness he could not fill with drugs or booze. He knew because he had damn near ended his own life through his overindulgence. Maybe that was why he'd been so willing to start that particular project. If even half of what they were saying was true, there would be danger and a chance of death. At one time, he would have fled, never to look back. But what did he have to lose now? Everything he'd thought he wanted to live for was gone. *Cancer!* Who would have thought someone so young, beautiful, and full of life could be absorbed so quickly and completely? The end had not been a curse; it had been a blessing. Her pain was over, and her fight, well fought, was now complete. Shawn hung his head and sobbed. If only he knew that she was all right, the soul carried on in some other plane, and she was happy and pain free, then maybe he could move on and live his life with some hope of seeing her again.

Shawn avoided his friends. After all, his friends had been her friends, and spending time with them was too hard. He could see the pity in their faces and their feeble attempts to act naturally around him. It was too much, so he spent more and more time alone. He knew that was not good. As for family, he hated his mother; she was a self-centered, egotistical bitch who thought of no one but herself. As for his dad, only the spineless remains of what had once been a proud and successful man were left. Spending time with them meant a good dose of biting his tongue. Just once, he wished he would tell his mother to fuck off. Shawn was an only child—a mistake, according to his mother, an unwanted burden to her. When Sam had died, there'd been no comfort from either of his parents, and they hadn't even come to the funeral. Shawn had made up his mind: he would live his life without them in it. He doubted they would even notice.

Shawn took his watch from the nightstand: 9:00 a.m. *Shit*, he thought. He had to be at Hoffman's in less than half an hour. Hoffman was a brute to work with, but Shawn had to admit he knew his stuff and was a stickler for details. Still, the way he treated his crew was horrific. Shawn remembered the time at the Winchester house when a young girl named Beth, on her first assignment, accidentally had erased a short piece of tape that Hoffman swore showed a shadow. "What the hell is the matter with you? Don't you have any brains? Get the hell out of here before you screw up something else!" he had raged. The girl had spent the rest of the day on the verge of tears and hadn't bothered to come back the next day. *What a prick*, thought Shawn.

Hurriedly, he jumped from his bed and pulled on his pants, shirt, and sandals. A shower was out of the question. He smelled his pits—not bad—and put on a heavy dose of Brut to cover any lingering odor. Phillip and Franky had promised him a ride, so he had five minutes to brush his teeth, comb his hair, and be out in front of the hotel.

Outside, the weather looked ominous. Storm clouds were brewing over his head, and the air was thick with the smell of rain. As he stood there, he pondered the characters who had come into his life over the last few hours. Joe seemed nice enough but almost too eager. Mary was nice enough, but her gazes at his crotch told him she tended to be a party girl. He did not judge her for that—hell, he had sown many wild oats at her age—but he also sensed in her a need for approval and maybe even a need to be loved. It could have just been his imagination, but she seemed sad somehow. Josette seemed nice, and he knew the two of them would get along fine. Shawn thought that behind her fragile frame, she could be a titan when called upon. Benjamin he liked; there was honesty in his demeanor, and Shawn was sure that any quarrels Benjamin had had with Hoffman were well deserved. He really liked Phillip; he thought him solid, with a quiet strength. With Franky, there'd seemed to be a natural bond from the moment they'd met. It was strange because Shawn always had been rather particular about whom he let into his life, even before he'd met Sam, but with Franky, it was different. They just seemed to jell in some way he could not explain. He was more than happy to finally see them pull up, and no sooner had he hopped into the back of Phillip's rental than the skies burst, and rain fell hard and heavy.

Once Shawn was inside, Franky turned from

the front seat. "Man, have we got some shit to tell you!"

As they entered the front door of Hoffman's flat, they saw Josette, Joe, and Mary sitting in the living room, having coffee. Josette must have filled everyone in, for as soon as they made it through the door, everyone started asking questions about what to do next. Should they venture to investigate the house after everything that had happened? Should they wait for Benjamin to be released from the hospital? Were the cops involved?

"Wait. Let's not get ahead of ourselves," said Phillip before he even reached the table.

"Where is Dr. Hoffman?" asked Franky.

"He went out. Didn't say where he was going," answered Mary.

"Does he know?" Phillip asked.

"No, I don't think so," responded Josette. "He was gone before I got here."

"Let's not make any decisions until we are all together," responded Phillip in his take-charge tone of voice.

"Look," said Mary, "I don't know how to take all this." With that, she got up and walked into the kitchen.

"How is Mr. Burk doing?" asked Joe sheepishly.

"Physically fine. They are only keeping him

for observation, but man, he went through a lot," said Franky.

Mary soon returned carrying the coffeepot and cups for the three new arrivals.

"Well then, at least now you all know that what we are up against is real," said Phillip. "Trust me, Franky and I can tell you much more. If you want out of this, get out now."

Josette at once turned her gaze to Joe, who gave no response. What power did Hoffman have over him? She knew he did not want to go through with the investigation, so why didn't he say anything?

"Okay, Dr. Hoffman," Mary said.

"Dr. Hoffman is not here," said Phillip sternly. "This is not a game, people; this thing is dangerous."

Just as Phillip was finishing his sentence, Hoffman came bursting in carrying a brown paper bag. On his face was a smile so broad it covered half his face. "Hello, everybody. I got us some bagels to start the day. I have my van packed with everything we will need, and the rain has stopped."

"We have some news," said Mary, avoiding looking into Hoffman's eyes.

"What?" he asked, the smile leaving his face as he looked at the face of everyone in the room. "What's going on?"

"Benjamin was attacked in his home last night," said Phillip.

"Fuck!" screamed Hoffman. He reached out and, with one swing, sent a table lamp flying across the floor. "Don't tell me we are not going to the house today. Don't fucking tell me that."

Everyone was shocked at his lack of concern, and their surprise was displayed openly on their faces.

"No, no, I have been waiting too long for this. We need to do this today," he said.

"Don't you even want to know if he is okay?" asked Shawn. "For God's sake, you don't even know if he's alive!"

Hoffman sat down on the couch, his face red with anger.

"He is getting out of the hospital this afternoon," said Franky.

"This is just great. I knew he would find a way to screw me," said Hoffman, not listening to anything else being said.

Finally, Phillip got up. "I think it is best we give Dr. Hoffman some time to compose himself." With that, he turned and walked to the door, looking at the rest of the group as if following him were not an option. Everyone got up and followed him out the door. Just outside, they could hear more things breaking inside.

"What a bloody asshole," said Josette.

Phillip gave her a smile.

With everyone still standing in the hall, there was an odd silence, as no one knew exactly what to do at that point.

"So what now?" asked Joe.

"I don't know about the rest of you, but I was up half the night, and to tell you the truth, I didn't sleep well even when I did finally fall asleep," said Phillip. "I am going back to my hotel room and getting some rest."

"I am all for that," Franky said.

"Me too," said Josette. It had been two in the morning by the time they'd gotten Benjamin to the hospital and three by the time he'd been admitted. The man had not said a word. Josette was sure he was in shock from the ordeal but would tell them all when he was ready. The only thing he'd managed to ask was how the three had even known he was there.

Franky had given him a one-word answer: "Josette."

Benjamin had asked for no further clarification.

"Someone will need to pick up Benjamin at the hospital this afternoon," said Franky.

"I'll go," responded Shawn. He seemed eager to assist in some way. "But I will need the use of your car, if that is okay."

"That would be fine," Phillip said.

"I could drive you," Joe told Shawn. "If that is okay with you. I feel like I need to do something."

"That will be great. I'm sure you know your way around better than I do," responded Shawn.

Everyone then seemed to instinctively turn his or her eyes to Mary.

"I am going to give him some time, and then I will come back to clean up the mess," she said unenthusiastically. "He'll calm down, and then he will be more reasonable, I'm sure." On her face was a look of doubt, but she seemed determined to smooth things over between Dr. Hoffman and the rest of the group.

Phillip turned to Josette. "Can we give you a lift back to your hotel?"

"I would like that," she said.

"Shawn?" asked Phillip.

"I can take him. That way, I know where to pick him up this afternoon," said Joe before Shawn could answer.

"That would be great," said Shawn.

With that, the group made their way to the elevators.

It was three o'clock in the afternoon when Phillip received the call from Mary. Dr. Hoffman was requesting the group reconvene at his house at six o'clock. He would provide a nice dinner. Phillip, hesitant at first, reluctantly accepted the offer. If it had not been for Mary's assurance that Dr. Hoffman was himself and truly felt bad about the way he'd acted, he would have declined. Phillip still had doubts. Maybe Hoffman was not stable enough for their mission. The thought made Phillip uneasy, to say the least. Still, he was willing to hear the man out. Shortly after he had ended the call from Mary, he received a call from Shawn. Shawn and Joe had just returned home with Benjamin; however, Benjamin was packing. He no longer wanted to stay at his manor and was moving to his flat in town. Phillip told him about Hoffman's invitation to dinner. After a short discussion among Shawn, Joe, and Benjamin that Phillip could barely make out over the phone, Shawn came back on the line and said that Joe and Benjamin would both be joining them. Phillip wondered if Shawn had let Benjamin in on Hoffman's behavior before he agreed. Regardless, the meeting that afternoon was set. Franky too was reluctant at first, but after some thought, he said, "We are wasting time. Whatever it takes."

Phillip thought about contacting Josette but was sure Mary had seen to that. He gave the girl a lot of credit; she seemed to always be on top of things. Phillip still could not believe that Hoffman was lucky enough to have her and that she stayed even after all the bullshit. Maybe she needed the money, or maybe she just wasn't one to give up easily.

Franky walked out of the bathroom with a towel wrapped around his waist. "It's amazing how Josette knew about Benjamin last night. Don't you think?" he said.

"Yes, she is an amazing woman," responded Phillip.

Franky dropped the towel; reached into the dresser drawer; pulled out a pair of underwear, pants, a shirt, and socks; and laid them on the bed. "I was skeptical at first about her so-called abilities, but man."

Phillip sat up in his bed. "She said a spirit told her. What did she call it?"

"Her spirit guide," said Franky, pulling on his tighty-whities.

"All I know is that she knew exactly where to find him. We never would have found that dungeon without her. She led us straight to the door."

"And she stormed down those steps like a trooper. I could tell she was terrified, but it seemed her willingness to save Benjamin overcame her fear. Remarkable."

Phillip nodded in agreement.

"Phillip, there is something I need to tell you," said Franky hesitantly. "I am not going back to Parksville University in the fall."

"Then you got the job in Ann Arbor. That's great," responded Phillip.

Franky looked shocked. "You knew?"

"You interviewed with Kissinger. We are old friends. I gave you a glowing reference, by the way."

"If you knew, why didn't you say something?"

"Well, I didn't know if you got it, only that you interviewed. I figured you would tell me once you knew for sure." Phillip paused, stood up, walked over to Franky, and gave him a big hug. "I am so proud of you."

Nothing else Phillip could have said would have made Franky feel so happy. "I will have to get a place and rent a truck."

"That's part of the fun; you get to find your own space," said Phillip. "Finally, you can get all that stuff out of storage."

As Franky finished getting dressed, his thoughts went to Sue Barkley, the girl he had helped move into Mrs. Cartwright's many years ago. He recalled the look of excitement on her face when she'd put things in just the right spots. He smiled. How lovely and how happy she'd been. He was amazed at how infatuated he had been with her—yes, even in love, he guessed—and then the beast had taken her away.

"I am heading down. Don't rush. I will pick you up out front," said Phillip. With that, he got up and walked toward the door, checking his pockets for his room key.

Josette was the first to arrive at Hoffman's. She'd hoped others would be there first to break the awkwardness, but as she entered, she received a warm welcome from Mary. Hoffman was still working in his den. Hopefully others would arrive before he emerged, she thought.

Softly, Mary whispered, "He feels ever so bad about what happened."

Josette offered her a smile and took her seat at the large dining room table. A few minutes later, there came a knock on the door; Joe, Shawn, and Benjamin had arrived. A feeling of relief came over her; she would not have to face Dr. Hoffman alone.

Benjamin walked over, took her hand in his, and kissed it softly. "I owe you my life."

"I wouldn't go that far."

"I would," he said, taking the seat next to her at the table.

"You know, from the moment I saw you, you looked awfully familiar to me. Have we met before?" Josette asked Benjamin.

"Yes, in London. A benefit ball, as I recall."

"Now I remember. It was the Scotland Yard Benefit Ball for Children," she said. Josette was glad to see he had recovered from last night's events. "So glad to see you in better health this evening."

No sooner had Joe and Shawn taken their seats than Phillip and Franky arrived. Still, there was no sign of Hoffman.

Phillip sat next to Josette on the opposite side of Benjamin. "Well," he said to both of them, "that was quite a night."

Josette smiled at him, and Benjamin offered a look of gratitude.

"Now that things have calmed down slightly," Phillip said, looking straight at Josette, "tell us more about how you knew Benjamin was in such dire straits."

"My spirit guide," she responded. "This one only came to me a short while ago, but I think it is the most powerful one I have ever had. It has a passion I have never felt."

"Who is this guide?" asked Shawn.

"I do not know yet," she answered, "but I know I trust it completely. It's a feeling I have deep down. This guide wishes only to protect us against this evil. I am sure Phillip and Franky can relate. Did you not have a guide with your experience in the States? A priest, I believe you said. Spirit guides are not like those spirits that do not go on into the light and remain in this world when they die. They have traveled on, but for some reason, they need to break through from their world to this one, and that takes time and unrelenting effort. I am sure that when the priest first made contact with you, you had no idea who or what it was. Am I correct?"

"Yes, you are a hundred percent correct," responded Phillip.

"Are you a medium too?" Joe asked Phillip.

"Not me. That was a first and a last," Phillip responded.

"This guide appears in solid white," Josette said. "Until it is ready or able to show itself, I need to trust that what it tells me is true. It said clearly that Mr. Burk was in danger and that if help was not given right away, he would not be with us for the rest of this little adventure, and we would never be successful without him."

"Do you know if this guide is male or female from its voice?" Shawn asked.

"No, not yet. Communication with this guide is sometimes complicated. It is more of a feeling and sometimes a vision. Eventually, I am hoping to communicate directly, but I can't yet."

Mary, who had been sitting quietly in the background, looked somewhat skeptical of the whole thing. "What does the guide say about killing this thing?"

"Nothing," said Josette somewhat defensively. She had spent her life dealing with people who thought she was a fraud and did not believe. "It has told me many things but only what it chooses to." In fact, the guide had told her many different kinds of things, and that was why she had agreed to the adventure to start with. She had known in advance that Hoffman would contact her, and she also knew that her participation would mean life or death for the group. She also had been told that for the first time, she would know true love, and her life would never be the same. That information she would keep to herself. It was meant for no one else; it was for her alone.

Mary was just getting ready for her follow-up question, when Hoffman came bounding into the room. An oversize smile was planted on his face. "Friends, I am so glad you came, and I do want ever so much to apologize for my behavior earlier."

"Jekyll and Hyde," whispered Franky to Shawn, who grinned in agreement.

"Please, let's have dinner. We will discuss this investigation after with some brandy."

Throughout dinner, Hoffman continued with the apologies, and for the most part, they seemed authentic enough to the group—that was, to everyone but Benjamin, who sat quietly and never responded to any of Hoffman's attempts at atonement. After dinner, everyone moved back into the living room. They had just gotten comfortable, when Hoffman asked the question he had been containing with all his will.

"What about the investigation of the house?" He spoke to no one in particular.

"I have got to go into that house," Josette said, not waiting for anyone else to respond. "There is something there. I can feel it. I have to go."

Phillip was impressed with her directness. Even as she spoke, he knew that going into that house frightened the shit out of her; he could sense it in her voice.

"I agree," said Benjamin. "We need answers, and that house is the only thing we have to go on."

The look on Hoffman's face was one of pure contentment. Not only had Josette said the investigation must be done, but Ben had agreed. He'd thought he had lost his chance, but his last-ditch effort had paid off.

"I am going to my flat in town after this meeting," Benjamin said. "I want tomorrow to recover and bring some things I require to the flat for my extended stay. I want Josette to accompany me to the house, if she would be so kind. Maybe Phillip as well for some added security. In the meantime, I think Hoffman and his crew should go prepare the house with all their cameras and eletro-whatevers. At least that will give us one night to monitor it before we go in."

Everyone paused, waiting for Hoffman's reaction.

"I think that is a great idea," said Hoffman to

everyone's amazement. "Joe, Shawn, and I can get everything set up in the morning. Dr. Lake, we could sure use the extra help, if you would be so kind."

Franky nodded in agreement.

"Great. We have a plan," said Hoffman.

CHAPTER 6

A NEW FLAME

Sitting alongside the road in his bloodstained stolen car, Mathew Duryee clung to life by a thread. After the police had passed by unknowingly, Mathew had pulled his luxury car out of its hiding space and driven out of town. Once safely in the countryside, he'd found a spot well hidden from the main road and stopped. He could not go on. As the sunlight faded, he knew that if his wounds were not attended to soon, he would die. He could have gone to the hospital right off, but he knew once he did, there would be an investigation. They would know right off who he was, and he would spend the rest of his life behind bars. He had been careful to be, in his mind, a model citizen despite the murders. He lived alone on his yacht, a nice sloop that he always kept anchored away from everyone else. Unless he was on a job, he was on the sea. He never broke any traffic laws, got intoxicated, caused any disturbance, or did anything to bring him in touch with the law. Sure, he had left his DNA at murder scenes; one couldn't do what he did the way he did it and not leave a little of himself behind. Still, if he was never arrested, fingerprinted, and made to give a sample, he was free. To live in a cage was no life at all. He was not afraid of the people; he feared the confinement.

This was to be his last hit—the final bow, as it were—and then he was to go off on his boat to paradise, never to venture out of sight of the Southern Cross again. The boat was already loaded with everything he would need for his trip and then some. He'd planned it all so well, right from the theater to his boat. He'd planned to be out to sea, never to be seen or heard from again. How quickly that all had changed.

Fear overwhelmed him as the realization of death filled him. Maybe he'd made his choice not to seek medical help, to pick death rather than confinement, too quickly, but he was beyond the point of turning back now. He did not have the strength to move, and his breathing was becoming shallower. He was dying, and nothing could change that.

From behind him, he heard the rear car door open, and someone got in the back. The stench was overwhelming, and he started to feel sick to his stomach. He tried in vain to muster the strength to turn to no avail. From behind him, he heard, just above a whisper, "You have a choice to make, my friend."

Franky and Shawn had agreed to stay with Benjamin for the night in case anything else should happen, but first, they decided to venture down to the pub to toss a few, and Mary and Joe eagerly agreed to join them. As for Phillip, he had no desire to go to any pub, and neither did Josette; they agreed to go out for dessert and coffee. Hoffman, who graciously declined their offer to join them, recommended a nice, quiet diner right down the street. As the party parted ways at the bottom of the steps, Phillip and Josette said their goodbyes and then turned to the left and strolled up the street, while the rest climbed into Joe's car.

The warm summer night was oddly quiet along the busy stretch of road.

"Josette, I am sorry, but I have to ask why you are here."

"Excuse me?" she said.

"What made you come to Dublin? Why did you agree to help Dr. Hoffman?"

She turned her eyes away from Phillip. "I have my reasons; mostly, it was because of the things my spirit guide showed me."

"Forgive me, but I have a strong feeling there is a lot more to this than what you are saying."

She offered Phillip a smile. "You are a smart man, Phillip. I will be more than happy to tell you everything after this ordeal is past us. I do want to tell you one thing I know, and I have not shared it with the group because I do not know whom to trust. There is one in the group who will try to betray us all. The guide was very adamant about that. I would be careful."

"So why are you telling me?" asked Phillip.

"Because I trust you, Phillip. I don't know why, but I know you are a man to be trusted."

"Well, I thank you for your confidence," he said, offering her a smile.

"Do you know who it might be?" she asked.

"Well, I know Franky is out of the question. As for the rest, they are really strangers to me. I mean, I don't really know any of them, do I?" asked Phillip.

"We will need to keep our eyes open. I wish I knew more facts. I hate it when I only get pieces of the puzzle," Josette replied. "My guide would not disclose who."

The diner was quaint, and the cheesecake was amazing. Sitting alone at a small table with a red tablecloth and white candles burning in wide glass bowls, they found themselves at ease, enjoying each other's company. Outside the large window where they sat, crowds of people walked by as if there were nothing in the world to worry about.

"Let's make a deal," said Phillip, raising his coffee cup. "Let's not talk about Banthom tonight or anything to do with the case."

Josette raised her cup. "Agreed, and for God's sake, don't mention the name Hoffman again tonight. That man is getting under my skin."

They took turns throwing jabs at Hoffman, imitating him in sarcastic ways. They giggled like school kids.

"How is it a beautiful girl like you is still single?" asked Phillip without warning, catching Josette off guard.

She smiled and thought for a while before responding. "I never found my soul mate, I guess," she said, looking up from her coffee.

"Surely many have tried to court you."

"Most men are afraid of me," she said, gazing out the window. "They think I am a freak because of how I earn a living. Or they think I can somehow read their minds or tell their futures. I am a medium, not a mind reader. I talk to dead people—that's all I do. How or why I have this gift I don't know, but there it is. I am not going to hide it and pretend to be someone I am not. I did that long enough. It's hard to fit in sometimes. It's like I don't really fit in anywhere."

"You seem to fit into this group fairly well," said Phillip, grabbing the check.

"Well, let's face it. This is not your average group of people. I mean, we are looking at hunting a flesh-eating witch. That's not like having a few friends over for tea."

"Well, I would have you for tea anytime," he responded with a huge grin.

"I know you would. That's what makes you so special, Phillip: you accept people for who they are. I have the feeling you'd be the same man talking to some poor beggar on the street as you would be conversing with the queen herself."

Phillip thought that was one of the greatest compliments he had ever received. He liked all people regardless of age, economic standing, race, religion, or sexual orientation. Deep down, he found people fascinating. He firmly believed that most people were good and that if given the chance, anyone could be a friend.

After dessert, Phillip and Josette walked back to Hoffman's to retrieve his rental. She had agreed to let him take her back to her hotel. Josette found the night magical and perfect. The thought of the evil things that had happened escaped her. She had no doubt Phillip was the one her spirit guide had spoken of, the one who would make her life complete. As they pulled in front of her hotel, she turned to Phillip.

"I have never asked this of a man before," she said, avoiding his eyes, "but would you like to come up to my place for a nightcap?"

Phillip smiled back at her and surprised himself when he said, "I would love nothing more."

Franky sat back and enjoyed the show. Once intoxicated, both Mary and Benjamin started speaking in such thick Irish accents that Shawn, Joe, and Franky could not follow. Joe got up, made a toast to their adventures to come, and gave a loud whoop into the smoke-filled air. Though Franky joined in the toast, he knew the investigation would not be something to look forward to. The situation was far more serious than any of them knew. Around one o'clock in the morning, the party ended. Mary and Joe left at the same time, while Shawn and Franky waited patiently on Benjamin; it seemed the man knew everyone and was quick to buy a round for the pub, which only heightened his popularity.

Upon arriving at Benjamin's flat in town, Franky was once again in awe. His house was impressive, but his flat was amazing. It was done in white, including the walls, carpet, and curtains. The furniture was all plush black leather, with white throw pillows everywhere. A large, circular stairway in the middle of the room went up to the second floor. The living room and bar had a two-story ceiling, with long-paned glass windows on the far wall going up to the full height of the rooms. The windows gave a magnificent panoramic view of the city. Up the stairway, Franky saw an open walkway to several rooms, with a banister running the length of the upper floor. There were at least six bedrooms. Under the floor of the upper level and directly behind the living room was the kitchen. It was so clean that it shone under the florescent lighting, and Franky was amazed at the different gadgets it held. Still on the first floor, behind the bar was yet another door, leading to what was obviously the master bedroom. It was amazing.

Once inside, Benjamin walked nonchalantly into the kitchen, grabbed the salt, and left a thick layer in front of the door. "The windows are already done, so you can sleep tight," he said.

"We are on the fifteenth floor. Do you really think it can reach us up here?" asked Shawn.

"Yes," responded Franky before Benjamin could say a word. "I have no doubt that bastard could reach us anywhere it wanted." Franky spoke without looking at either one of them, choosing instead to turn his gaze to the floor. The certainty in his voice made the two men take pause.

"Shit," said Shawn. "That's not heartening."

"I've seen what this thing can do. The only blessing we have is that it doesn't know anything about the rest of us. At least as far as we know, it doesn't, but trust me, that won't take long. These fuckers have a way of knowing things. It knows about Benjamin—that we know for certain—and that is enough to take every precaution. I have little doubt that if it finds him again, it will not stop until it has all the information it needs."

"Well, let's not dwell on that tonight. Make yourselves at home. It'll be a long day tomorrow," Benjamin said. He walked into his room and shut the door.

Shawn and Franky looked at each other. "Well, I guess we have our pick," said Shawn, looking up at all the rooms on the second floor.

"Can you believe this fucking place?" asked Franky.

"Man, this man has more money than he knows what to do with," Shawn said.

"No shit. Just look at this view," Franky said, turning to the windows. "Man, I could live like this."

Shawn walked over to the fully stocked bar. "Want a nightcap? He has everything you can imagine here."

"Anything I can see through?" joked Franky. He'd had his fill of Guinness.

"How about a Bacardi and Coke?"

"That sounds like a winner."

Shawn returned with the drinks to the living

room, where Franky had taken residency on the sofa. "Mary was giving you the eye tonight."

"Bullshit," said Franky. "She was all over Benjamin. Hell, what woman wouldn't be?"

"Nah, a lot of the time, she was looking at you, my friend."

"You're delusional. Besides, I am not interested."

"Why? She's hot," said Shawn, a little shocked.

"I'll give you that," said Franky, "but I don't think she is what I am looking for right now."

"God knows Joe was giving it all he had. Did you see the way he followed her around the pub? Man, that guy's got it bad. It was almost sad to watch, and she acted like he wasn't even alive," Shawn said.

"What about you? I saw her eyeing you once or twice," said Franky, smiling.

"No, I am still getting over someone. I don't think I am ready. I like Mary; she is a nice girl. A little on the wild side, but under other circumstances, I would be asking her out."

"So who was this girl who dumped you?" Franky asked jokingly.

"Her name was Samantha. I just called her Sam," Shawn replied, hanging his head down so he was looking at his shoes.

"What happened?" Franky asked, working hard to pull his foot out of his mouth. Obviously, something terrible had taken place.

"Cancer. She died about six months ago," responded Shawn.

"Oh man, I am so sorry. I didn't know."

"It's okay. I just think it will take a while, you know," Shawn responded with a forced smile.

Franky's thoughts went to Sue Barkley, his first real love, who had been taken by the beast Fritz. "Yeah, I know," he said.

As Joe entered his apartment, he had the strangest feeling of being watched. With all the talk of satanic worshippers and witches, there was good cause to be a little jumpy, but he still had his doubts about the whole affair, and in his current state, he doubted anything would scare him. He was willing to take on the world—at least until the booze wore off. He'd even had the guts to talk to Mary. Even if she'd been less than receptive, she still had been polite. He recognized that a girl like her would never go for a guy like him. He was not the hunky type, and even he did not like seeing himself naked. His mother always told him it was the person inside who counted, but he knew people looked at the outside before they ever thought of looking at the inside. Joe remembered how painful high school had been for him. He'd spent most of his time avoiding the school bully, Freddy Johnson. Gym class had been the worst;

they'd had to shower every day or get a bad mark for the day. Joe hadn't cared; he would take the bad grade even if that meant dealing with his father when the report card came. He'd made the mistake of going into the showers once, and Freddy, in front of all the other boys, had asked if he could play with his tits. "Bet they feel like the real thing," he had said, reaching over and giving one of them a squeeze. "Holy shit, I would fuck these titties!"

Joe had tried to return to his gym locker, but Freddy had blocked his way. "Hey, dude, what happened to your cock? Do you even have one under those rolls?" Freddy had said, laughing. "Pull up those rolls. Let's see if you even have a dick." Joe had tried to get around him, but it had been no use. "I said pull up those rolls, and let's see if you have a dick," Freddy had demanded.

In front of the whole class, Joe had been forced to lift his belly, exposing his insignificant package. The laughter that had followed haunted Joe to that day. The next day, as he'd walked down the halls, he'd been sure the other kids were pointing and laughing. Why had God been so mean to give him rolls, man boobs, and a small penis? *What did I do to deserve this?* thought Joe. Now, as a man, he avoided anyplace someone might see him nude. When using the men's room, he avoided the urinals, even if the stalls were full. He would wait.

Still, if only he could be given the chance, he

would show Mary what a man he could be. If only she could see past the wrapping. Before he even got all the way inside his small living room, he heard the sound of wind blowing through an open window in his bedroom. "Shit," he said aloud. He had left it open all day. He closed the window and made his way to his bed. He knew he had a long day ahead of him, and he crawled onto the bed fully clothed. At least tomorrow he would see her again; that was the only reason he had chosen to stay. As the room started spinning, he thought he could hear the wind rushing through the open window once more.

Phillip awoke with Josette nestled against his back. Quietly, he began to rise from the bed, only to be pulled back down.

"And just where do you think you're going? Got lucky, and now you're sneaking out," she said with a big smile on her face.

"Damn, you caught me!" Phillip joked. "I left a twenty on the nightstand. What else do you want?"

"I want you, you Yankee bastard," she replied.

"Well, I don't think we have time for another round this morning," he said, looking at his watch. "We are due at Burk's in twenty minutes."

"Shit!" Josette exclaimed, jumping out of bed. "What time is it?"

"Twenty to nine."

"I never sleep this late," she said, making her way to the bathroom and closing the door.

"Maybe I wore you out."

"Don't think so highly of yourself, Professor Parker," she replied from behind the door.

Phillip got up and pulled on his underwear. "I was hoping to go back to my hotel to change, but I don't know if there's time."

"Damn right there's time. I don't want to have to explain why you're wearing the same clothing as yesterday. I will call Benjamin to tell him we are going to be late. Now, get your ass going."

Phillip finished getting dressed and then knocked on the bathroom door and said, "I will be back in a flash."

"You'd better be," Josette replied.

Phillip smiled and left. As he walked into the morning air, he felt better than he had in years. He felt young again, as if he could conquer the world. He'd spent too long watching the world go by. He was tired of being a bystander. Maybe it was time he joined in the parade instead of watching from the curb.

He had only truly been in love twice in his life, but he knew he was falling hard for Josette. Everything about her just seemed right—the way she smiled, her wit, the way she listened intently to every word. However, the most important thing about her was her honest yet caring nature. She reminded him of Martha. Maybe that was why he was falling so fast and hard. He hoped she felt the same.

Back at the hotel, he had just gotten in the shower, when he heard the door to the room shut. Franky was back. If Franky had returned a few minutes earlier, he would have caught Phillip coming in, and then he would have known Phillip had not come back last night.

"Aren't you due at Benjamin's?" Franky said when he heard Phillip through the door.

"Overslept!" he yelled back. "What time you meeting at the house?"

"At ten. Are you about done? Shawn is coming right back. He's grabbing his things, checking out of his hotel, and staying at Benjamin's. He is waiting to get there to get ready, and then we are leaving from there."

Phillip shut off the shower. "All yours."

"Benjamin asked if we would like to stay there as well. Man, you should see that place. It's like nothing I've ever seen before."

Phillip came out in his towel. "That's up to you. Do you want to stay there?"

"Yeah, I think we should. God knows he's got the room."

"Sounds good to me," Phillip said.

"You sound rather upbeat this morning. Everything okay?"

"Couldn't be better. You take your shower, and I will pack our stuff. You can check us out when Shawn gets here. Deal?" Phillip said.

"Awesome. Wait till you see this place," said Franky as he walked into the bathroom and shut the door.

Phillip swiftly emptied the dressers and put all his clothes in his suitcase and all of Franky's in his duffel. Franky could get the toiletries and anything else left behind.

"Will you bring the luggage over?" he yelled through the door.

"Sure, I'll get it! Shawn can help!" Franky yelled back.

Phillip could not remember the last time he'd had to yell through a bathroom door, but that day, it was becoming the norm.

By the time he returned to Josette's hotel, she was already outside waiting.

Phillip rolled down his window as he pulled up next to her. "Young lady, may I give you a lift?"

"Well, okay, but I usually don't take rides from strangers," she replied as she got into the car.

The ride to Burk's place was quiet, but it was not a strange, awkward silence—more of a comfortable, at-ease stillness. More than once, they glanced at each other and smiled. Phillip thought

Josette seemed happy with the situation and what had happened last night. He put his hand in hers, and she gripped it tenderly. Then, out of blue, she said, "I really like you, Phillip."

"I really like you too," he responded. "You know, I am a good bit older than you."

"I know," she said, "but somehow …" She hesitated. "I don't know. This just feels so right."

They said nothing else until they reached Benjamin's apartment.

Chapter 7

THE BURK GHOST

Banthom House was situated on the hillside overlooking the town of Dalkey, which had acted as the harbor for Dublin back in the days of the Vikings and throughout most of the Middle Ages. In its day, the harbor would have been filled with large Anglo-Norman ships bringing goods from the rest of the known world.

Hoffman was the first to arrive at the house. In the early morning mist, it looked like a cottage from a fairy tale. It did not look at all ominous; rather, it looked serene. It seemed out of place in the more modern neighborhood; its gray stone walls and red-framed windows with matching shutters gave the impression it was somehow perched somewhere in the countryside, far beyond city streets. Though it had obviously undergone many restorations, it kept its box-shaped historical appearance. *It is like stepping back in time*, thought Hoffman.

He had seen it many times from the road. It loomed above the stone walls surrounding the property, but only the top-floor windows and the slanted roof were visible. Now, as he stood at the front door, it seemed underwhelming, as if the house were nothing more than that: a house. Generations had come and gone since Banthom, and there were never any reports of ghosts or demons that he could find; still, something about the place drew him to it. There were answers there, and he was going to find them. As he fit the key Benjamin had given him the night before into the door lock, a rush came over him. After all the dirty deeds he had done and all the lies and arguments to get to that point, it was finally at his fingertips. With one turn of the key, he would be inside.

Just as the lock clicked, Hoffman heard a car come up the drive. It was Joe; he too had arrived early. "Damn!" said Hoffman. He had hoped to be the first in the house to spend a little time getting a feel for the place. No sooner had Joe's car come to a stop than Mary pulled up. Hoffman ignored them both and went inside.

The door opened into a dining room off to the left, with a stairway running right up the middle of the ground floor. To the right was an outdated kitchen with an older-looking stove and oven on the side. Beyond the stairway was the living room, complete with a fireplace on the far wall. White sheets covered the furniture, but their shapes left little to the imagination as to what they were: a dining room table and chairs, a couch and love seat, and a credenza along the wall next to the back door. For a moment, Hoffman tried to imagine what it would have looked like back in the eighteenth century, with women dressed in fancy gowns and petticoats and men in their waistcoats and breeches.

"Dr. Hoffman, are you ready for us to start unloading?" Joe's meek voice asked from the front door.

"Yes, yes, let's get to it."

On the way to Burk's house, Phillip, Josette, and Benjamin decided to make a stop for coffee and a quick bite. They found a small mom-and-pop restaurant just off the main road and stopped. As they sat in the restaurant, Benjamin showed obvious tension about going back to the place where just a day before he'd been held captive with an iron cage on his head and a starving rat as his companion. He had not said much that whole morning, which was not common for him. More than once, Josette caught him running a finger along the wound Banthom had given him on his face.

"We still need to hear all you know about this," said Josette. "Remember, you were to brief the group on the background." She was trying to divert the man's attention away from the task ahead.

"I will make a point of doing just that this afternoon when we meet back at my flat," he responded. "I have told Phillip, Shawn, and Franky a lot about it, but I keep forgetting the rest of you were not there."

Phillip, after finishing his eggs, pushed his plate away and said, "That hit the spot."

Josette gave him a big smile.

"My God, you two did the nasty, didn't you?" blurted Benjamin.

"What are you talking about?" responded Phillip, not looking directly at Benjamin.

"Oh please, you two have been giving each other the eye all day, and Josette has been practically beaming all day. You two have done it. I know," joked Benjamin.

Josette giggled. "So what if we did?"

"I knew it," responded Benjamin.

"Please, let's keep this between just us. I really think it's best for now," said Phillip.

"My lips are sealed," responded Benjamin with a huge grin covering his face. "So if you don't mind me asking, and even if you do, I need to know: Are you two an item now?"

Phillip and Josette looked at each other with looks of anticipation, each waiting for the other to respond first.

"I hope so," said Phillip at last.

"Me too," Josette said, squeezing his arm.

"Brilliant! I don't know how, but you two seem to fit so nicely together," Benjamin said reassuringly as he finished his second cup of coffee.

"We did last night," said Josette with a devious grin.

Benjamin burst out laughing, and the redness of Phillip's face only made him laugh even harder.

"So what are our plans when we get there?" asked Phillip in an obvious attempt to change the subject.

"I need to make sure the manuscript is there and bring it with us. I don't think we have a chance without it," said Benjamin.

At once, Josette saw the look of concern come back to Benjamin. She looked over at Phillip, and it was noticeable that he too had perceived the man's sudden change in mood.

"It's going to be okay, Benjamin," said Josette. "If he is anywhere near the house, I am sure I will be able to feel his presence. We can always turn around if things don't seem right."

"I honestly don't think he will return to the

house. What he was looking for was not there, and that place cannot hold any pleasant memories for him," Benjamin said, and then he paused before continuing. "You know, I knew they brought him to that dungeon and tortured him."

"I never knew they did that. Is it in the manuscript?" asked Phillip.

"No, that's the one thing they never told the priest McDonald when he came back from England in search of Banthom. Besides, the townspeople dragged him off when they got no answers about their families, and the Burks never really knew what they did with him after they took him away. They did not lie; they just did not tell him everything. Besides, Banthom told me as much when we were in the dungeon."

"You must be careful. His is evil and a liar," said Josette.

"No, I knew it was true. I could feel it in his voice. God only knows what things they did to him down there. I mean, the people wanted to find out about their family members. They could have done anything. Throughout the centuries, torture items have been added to that dungeon, mostly for memorabilia. Who knew they might have actually been used in my own house?"

"Have no sympathy for the son of a bitch ever. Do you hear me?" said Phillip in a stern voice while slamming his fist on the table. "This thing has a pact with the devil himself, and if you are not careful, it can take away all you love and all you care for."

Everyone in the restaurant turned to see what the fuss was about. Josette smiled back to show that everything was fine.

"You don't understand. I have no compassion for Banthom," Benjamin responded more quietly. "But the place I have lived my whole life, the place I have felt loved and safe, now—"

"It will be again," said Josette. "This evil will pass."

"You know, my whole life I have been burdened with this strange family history of witches and evil doings. I never really believed it, but now that I know it's true and that I am actually a part of it, I have a strange feeling that as the story ends, so do the Burks."

Phillip, who by that time had regained his full composure, grabbed Benjamin by the wrist. "You and your family did not ask for this, and you were not part of some master plan. Don't let your fears take hold of you. He will use them against you. Trust me. I know."

Franky was feeling useless. He had helped carry in all the equipment, and both vehicles were now empty. Hoffman had directed traffic, saying,

"This goes here, and that goes there." He was so focused that he didn't even notice it was well past lunchtime. Joe and Shawn were busy angling this camera and that one, putting gadgets in certain spots throughout the house, and checking for cold spots. Franky had no idea how to help at that point. He made his way out of the house and found Mary sitting on the hood of Joe's car, petting a large black cat.

"Looks like you found a friend," he said.

"Yeah, she has been hanging out all morning. Funny, she seems to follow me wherever I go."

"Well, she does look like one smart cat," Franky said with a grin.

"Off with you now," said Mary as she placed the cat on the ground, but it just sat there, unmoving. "See?"

"I see she is fond of you," Franky said.

"Okay, Mr. Lake," Mary said, changing her demeanor, "what's your deal?"

"Excuse me?" Franky said, a little surprised.

"Are you gay, married, engaged, or what?"

"I am not following you at all on this," he responded.

Mary smiled and walked over to where Franky was leaning on the front of the house. She found a spot next to him and mimicked his stance. "I mean, I have been throwing myself at you for the past two days, and I'm getting nothing. I am starting to take it personally."

Franky gave her a big smile. It was clear she was only partly joking. "I'm sorry. You are a very beautiful woman. I know this sounds corny as hell, but, well, I'm just looking for something—I don't know—long term. Something forever."

"Shit, you're looking for a wife?" Mary exclaimed.

"Yeah, I guess I am. I want a family—you know, kids and stuff," he said, shrugging.

"And you think I'm not the marrying kind. Is that it?"

Franky smiled. "I think you are very much the marrying kind. But are you looking for that kind of commitment right now?"

"Fuck no! I am having the time of my life, but I wanted to make sure that when you looked at me, you thought I was someone you would consider marrying."

"You have my word on that," he said.

"Well, I guess that's that," she said as she bent over and dusted off her knees.

"Are you mad at me?" said Franky with a pouting face.

"No, I guess not. Honestly, I like a man who knows what he wants and not someone who can be manipulated into something he doesn't. Still, there's nothing wrong with having fun while you're looking."

"True, but I think I am at a point where fun and desire could become blurred with commitment. Does that make sense?"

"Yes, you're afraid you'd fall head over heels in love with me, and I would just throw you away like an old shoe. I can see where you might fear that, especially the part about falling madly in love with me." Mary smiled and gave him a big hug.

"Friends?" Franky asked.

"Good friends, I have a feeling," said Mary, smiling and giving him another big hug. She turned and walked into the house with the cat following close behind.

"Ask Hoffman if we can break for lunch!" yelled Frank.

"It's coming. I ordered it twenty minutes ago. I hope you like Chinese," she replied from inside.

As she entered the Burk estate, Josette was at once overwhelmed by its majesty. She had been in large estates before, but none had had that mix of Victorian modesty and modern aspects of color and light. The other night had been a rescue mission, but now she had time to take it all in. As she made her way through the house to the main stairway, her eyes scanned every corner.

She noticed a presence peeking behind different locations: over the upstairs banister, behind the grandfather clock in the front hall, and once from the drawing room door. She felt no ill intent from the entity, so she remained silent. For a house that long-standing, it was not surprising to find a lingering spirit.

"If you don't mind, I am going upstairs to my room to check on the manuscript. I will be right back," said Benjamin.

"Off with you then," said Josette.

Phillip smiled in agreement as Benjamin bounded up the steps. Phillip casually walked over to the velvet-seated bench and sat down. "Isn't this place something?" he said to Josette, who was in the process of sauntering over to join him.

"It's amazing, but I could never live in a place this big. I don't care how many maids, cooks, or other staff I had. It just doesn't seem like a home to me."

"Funny, I thought the same thing the first time I walked through this door. I mean, it's beautiful— that's for sure—but what does someone do with all this empty space?"

"I wonder what someone who grew up in a house like this would do if forced to live in a single-bedroom flat like mine." Josette had a slight smile as she tried to picture it in her mind.

"Where would the butler sleep?" joked Phillip.

"I don't know. How good looking is he?" replied Josette.

After about five minutes, Benjamin came bounding down the stairs with the manuscript in one hand and a duffel in the other. "Good thing he didn't know what this is," he said. "Now I have to go into the drawing room."

"Why the drawing room?" Josette asked.

"I know this sounds obscene, but I need to see if he touched the family jewels," answered Benjamin. "The family has kept a safe in the drawing room for the past hundred years."

Just then, Josette saw the hidden figure as it walked from the drawing room into the kitchen. It was a large, dark figure, and this time, it made no attempt to stay hidden from Josette. He was dressed as a priest, complete with a black robe and collar, and his hair was as red as the evening sun. He gave a pleading glance in her direction. "I'll be right back. I need to get a drink of water," she told the men. As Phillip followed Benjamin into the drawing room, Josette followed the shadowy figure into the kitchen. There he stood, his face showing the need to show her something. He pointed to a far door. Josette knew the door all too well, for it was the door to the dungeon. She was not sure how she knew, but she was certain the apparition was a Burk. She felt the hairs on her neck rise as he slowly opened the door and motioned for her to enter. She looked at the spirit's face and saw a look of nobility and quiet assurance.

Phillip could have told her just what the man had looked like when young and full of life, for he was staring once again at the portrait in the drawing room of Marcus Burk. Phillip was once again struck by the man's look of authority.

"Dear Marcus was the protector of not only the Grand Grimoires but also the family treasures," said Benjamin, pushing a button on the majestic hand-carved frame. The picture swung open, exposing a wall safe behind it. "I know it's old-fashioned, the old safe behind the picture, but here is something new I have added."

On the safe was a black pad where Benjamin placed his thumb. A bright light scanned his print, and the safe popped open. Benjamin had not been lying: the inside was filled with jewels. A large diamond-laid tiara with an oversize sapphire in the center sat on top of hundreds of jewelry boxes, all neatly stacked and labeled.

"Throughout the centuries, the Burks have kept their jewelry in this safe, most only to be worn on certain occasions. The Burks never bury their jewelry with their dead, as that is viewed as a sign of vanity to God," he said with a grin. "It also protected the family assets, if you know what I mean. Whether out of greed or religious beliefs, it does not truly matter. Over time, it has evolved into quite a collection."

"So what is a collection like this worth?"

"Last time, it was appraised at more than four million dollars," said Benjamin as if it were no big deal. "Of course, that was more than ten years ago. The nice thing about jewels is that they increase in value."

From the stack of boxes, Benjamin pulled one that seemed specially placed on top of the stack. "This I will be wearing until this matter is resolved."

As he opened it, Phillip saw the same ring that Marcus wore in the painting: a large bloodred ruby perched upon a band of solid gold.

"This ring was given to the Burk family by the pope. It was to be a symbol of their dedication to protecting the books, and it was worn by every Burk chosen to join the church for generations, right up to and including Marcus. He was the last to wear it. Since then, no Burk has become a priest or nun. The mission was a failure, a dark spot on the Burk name. Still, under the guidance of Father McDonald, they continued to protect the secret because they alone have the task of finding both books and returning them to Rome. Why they were not taken there in the first place is beyond me."

"And my copy—you never said why you left the States without it."

"Even with a lot of help, I could not figure out where you kept it hidden. I even had your office searched but found nothing. I knew you had it well stashed, but I also knew I would find it eventually."

Just then, a loud scream came from the direction of the kitchen. It was Josette.

As the two men dashed into the kitchen, they noticed the door to the dungeon was open. They flew to it, and looking down the steps, they saw Josette sitting there laughing. "Sorry. I thought I could miss a step and get to the bottom faster," she said as they appeared at the top of the steps.

"What are you doing down there?" asked Phillip.

"I was guided down here by one of Benjamin's family members," she replied.

"What?" said Benjamin, still standing at the top of the stairs.

Phillip, who had reached the bottom, helped her to her feet. "Are you all right? Anything broken?"

"Just my dignity, as it were," she responded. "Benjamin dear, please do not come down here. If you could please just give me a minute. I know you are not ready to face this place."

"This is my house, and I'll be damned if anyone or anything will take that away from me." With that, he slowly descended the stairs. His eyes searched every inch of the visible dungeon. Even with the overhead light, it still had many dark, unseen corners.

"I'm sorry, Benjamin, but I feel there is something here I need to see," said Josette.

"I have been through this place a million times. I don't know what it is you're looking for, but maybe I can help," Benjamin said.

Josette looked around. To the right were low-arched doorways with the remnants of iron hinges still inserted deep into the brick sides. Slowly, she closed her eyes, and when she opened them again, the room was lit not by the glow of a bulb but by the soft glow of candlelight. On the far left, the same figure she had followed down into the darkness sat at a lone table. He was writing quietly, lost in thought. Out of the shadows, a hooded figured appeared from behind. The glow of the candlelight flashed off the shining blade of the knife lifted over his head. The priest never saw the blow coming; it landed squarely in the back of his neck. Without a sound, the priest crumpled to the cold stone floor. Without missing a step, the figure moved across the room to a large wooden chest on the floor next to the still-twitching body of the priest. Josette could feel the air grow cool as he opened the chest. The figure reached in and pulled out two large books. He then felt around the chest, and a sound of frustration escaped his lips. He'd expected to find something else. Something he'd hoped for was missing. Slowly and quietly, he closed the lid and made his way around the back of the dungeon.

"Josette?" She heard the calming voice of Phillip. "You okay?"

"Yes, I just saw something."

"You looked a little spaced out for a moment."

Josette turned and smiled at Phillip. The vision was now gone. Poor Phillip. He would need to get used to that behavior if he was going to be around her long.

"He knew what was here and where to find it," she said in the direction of Benjamin. "Your ancestor never had a chance. He knew."

"I'm sorry?" replied Benjamin, obviously still a little skittish.

"Your ancestor—the priest Marcus. He was murdered in this place over two books, but I think the murderer thought he would find more. A third maybe. Anyway, someone who knew him betrayed Marcus." Josette spoke as if she were once again in a trance. "I think it was another Burk or one of the staff, but he knew right where to look."

"Who was the man who killed him?" asked Phillip. "Banthom?"

"Bacon. The man who killed Marcus was named Bacon," she replied. "His spirit is dark. I can still feel his presence in this room."

"Shit," said Phillip. "That was the name of the

cult member—the Judas, they called him—whom
Fritz replaced. He's like the second-in-command,
you could say."

Josette saw the figure once again, this time at
the top of the steps leading back up to the kitchen.
From the doorway, the apparition smiled. "There
was nothing he could have done. That's what he
wanted to let me know—to let everyone know."
Josette smiled back, and then the figure vanished.
"It was not his fault."

By five o'clock that evening, the group in its
entirety was back in Benjamin's flat. They conveyed
to each other all the day's adventures. Hoffman
talked in detail about how well the house was
prepped with camera angles, motion detectors,
and sound-recording devices. Benjamin filled in
everyone who had not heard about his family
history and what Josette had seen that day. After
all those years, it turned out the death of Marcus
had been a matter of betrayal. Marcus had been set
up. For the first time, there seemed to be harmony
among all members of the group; they enjoyed
drink, laughter, and productive conversations.
Hoffman, still skeptical of the Burk family history
and all the talk of witchcraft, kept his doubts to
himself and at least pretended to be interested.

Mary and Benjamin worked on getting out the

food and drinks delivered from Benjamin's favorite takeout. Their laughter echoed in the kitchen area all the way to the bar and living room. Hoffman had all the details of the next day worked out and was telling them to Shawn, including who would ride with whom and what room they would start in. He'd planned the investigation right down to the smallest detail. He was like a kid planning his first trip to Disneyland.

Phillip and Josette walked into the living room and sneaked a kiss.

"So where is your copy of the book?" Josette asked Phillip.

Phillip, leaning on the back of a tall chair, looked around and softly answered, "It is with a dear friend in Florida."

"I've been to Florida a bunch of times," said Joe, who was sitting unseen on the other side of the chair. "I have family there."

"That's nice," said Phillip, surprised he was in the room.

Josette could not suppress a slight giggle.

"Come and get it!" Benjamin said from the dining area. "How is it you Americans would put it? Come get your vittles while they're still hot."

"Vittles? Really? You think Americans really talk like that?" Shawn laughed.

"Only backwoods rejects like you," Benjamin replied.

"Please. The only hills I travel have Beverly in front of the name," responded Shawn, and he snapped his fingers, trying not to laugh.

Dinner was pleasant. Franky and Phillip finally got to tell their tale of horror about what had occurred with the witch called Fritz. Everyone, excluding Hoffman, seemed enthralled by the tale but none as much as Benjamin, who seemed to hang on their every word. When they got to the part about losing family and friends, the group seemed to have a new respect for the odd pair of small-town educators. Josette, ignoring what anyone thought, reached under the table and grabbed Phillip's hand as he started to get emotional toward the end. There was a long pause after they were done speaking; even Hoffman seemed at a loss for words. Phillip finally said they needed to talk about something else; he and Franky had just wanted to remind them of what they were up against.

"Let's talk about where we are all from," said Josette, taking Phillip's lead. "Shawn, let's start with you. Tell us about what life is like in California." With that, the conversation moved to more pleasant subjects, with Shawn giving a pleasant description of his home.

After dinner, Joe said he wanted to get a picture of the group all together and left to get his Canon out of his car. The sun was close to setting, and the view from the flat was amazing because of the large open windows.

After about twenty minutes, the group was starting to worry about what was taking Joe so long. "Shall I go down to check on him?" Shawn said.

Before anyone could answer, Joe came bounding through the door with camera in hand.

Phillip watched as Benjamin reapplied a line of salt along the front door. He did so whenever anyone left or came back in. He was still scared; it was obvious by the way he obsessed over keeping the line unbroken.

"Hurry. We have the perfect light," said Shawn.

Joe hurried to set up the tripod, set the camera timer, and run back into the picture.

Click.

"One more," Joe said.

Suddenly, they all heard Mary's bloodcurdling scream. Everyone turned to see her staring at the window with her hand on her face, which looked as white as milk. "There was a fucking face in the window! I swear to God. A hideous face was staring right at me, right down there along the edge of the glass!"

Phillip ran to the window, looked down, and said, "There is nothing there now."

"Please. You're letting all this talk get to you.

We are fifteen floors off the ground, for God's sake," Hoffman said.

"I know what I saw. There was a man's face staring at me with big brown eyes. He wasn't human. He wasn't!" she snapped, holding back tears.

"Really, Mary, you need to get ahold of yourself," Hoffman said.

Franky jumped to her defense. "You all still have no idea, do you?" He spoke directly toward Hoffman. "This creature is not human, and if she says she saw it, then she saw it."

"Rubbish. It is a trick of the mind—nothing more," said Hoffman, raising his voice and taking a posturing stance.

"This thing can show you shit that will make you wish you were never born. Trust me. I know," Franky said. "Phillip and I told you from the first day that this thing is pure evil, and now it knows exactly who we all are."

"What's that?" asked Josette, looking out the window at a large, looming black ball floating on the wind.

"A storm cloud, by the looks of it," Hoffman huffed, dismissing everything Franky had just said.

"No, it's moving funny. Look. It's going up and down as it nears," said Benjamin.

"Joe, do you still have your camera?" asked

Shawn. "Come get a picture of this." He turned, but Joe was not there. Obviously, the whole situation had been too much for him.

"Fuck, it's coming pretty fast," said Shawn.

"It must be a mile away," said Hoffman.

The group looked on and saw that Shawn was right: it was moving quickly and seemed to be heading straight for them.

"It's just a flock of birds," said Hoffman.

For once, all of them agreed with him, for it was in fact a large gathering of blackbirds, and they were flying in a tight formation.

"Shit," said Phillip. "They're not stopping. They're coming straight for us." As he spoke, the enormous black-feathered mass blocked the last of the sun's rays.

As the group in Dublin were posing for a group photo, Brandy and Ethel were returning from Lake Wales along Florida's Highway 60. They had gone to Bok Tower for the plant sale that morning. Bok Tower was one of Brandy's favorite places. The shining carillon tower, with its golden door and the reflection pond, seemed like a place out of a Tolkien novel, surreal in its beauty and serenity. Ethel seemed far more taken with Pinewood Estate, a Mediterranean-style mansion built in the 1930s and nestled quietly just downhill from the tower.

No wonder Ethel liked it best, thought Brandy to herself; it was, like Ethel, strong, charming, mysterious, and classy.

They had gone to find plants for Ethel's newly installed and completely functional home next to Brandy's. They had bought four hibiscuses, Mexican petunias, a small sable palm, and a number of perennials they had agreed to plant in a shared garden between their houses. Brandy was sure they had spent more to drive to Lake Wales than they'd saved at the sale, but it was a nice day, and any trip to Bok Tower was worth it. They'd spent most of their morning walking the gardens, taking in their beauty. Though both complained about how their feet ached, both agreed it was a great trip.

All the way home, Brandy talked about life in Michigan, including the neighbors she'd liked and those she had not. She talked about how she missed the seasons, especially the fall, when the air cooled and the leaves turned. Without giving away too much information, she talked about the awful murders in Parksville and the lovely girl who'd been killed at Brandy's own home. "You know, it's funny, but all the time I was going through that ordeal, I wished you were there with me."

"Me? Why?" asked Ethel with a puzzled look on her face.

"Because I know you know about those things.

Sonny told me long ago that your family had a reputation for knowing about voodoo," Brandy said timidly.

"Honey, at one time, my family was the voodoo in New Orleans. Let's just say I walked away from all that when I was very young."

"Sonny said you had the gift, whatever that means."

"Sonny said a lot of things, most of it bullshit!" Ethel snapped.

"I'm so sorry. I didn't mean to upset you. I just wanted to let you know you were the one I wanted by my side when all that craziness took place. That's all. I needed my friend," Brandy said.

"I know. Sorry I yelled," Ethel said. "Listen, when I was just a child, they told me I had to take my place in the family. They said I was the gifted one. Throughout my childhood, they jammed all that nonsense down my throat. I hated it, every minute of it. I didn't want anyone telling me who I was or what I had to be." Ethel paused. "Do you know what I mean?"

"Please. If my parents had had their way, I would have spent my life driving a tractor and bailing hay! I know what you mean. Trust me," Brandy responded with a shiver. "When I think about what my life would have been ..."

"So you understand?"

"Please. When I got the chance, I got the hell off the farm and never went back," said Brandy.

After a long pause, Ethel said, "Please don't tell anyone about my past, Brandy. People look at you differently when they know."

"Not a word," said Brandy.

"Thanks," said Ethel with a smile. Ethel knew Brandy would keep her word if it killed her. There was no one in the world she trusted more than the woman behind the wheel. From the first time she'd met her that night at Moe's, she'd thought Brandy the most upfront and honest person she had ever met. You knew where you stood with Brandy. If you fucked up, she would let you know, and if you did well, she would let you know. If she liked you, you knew it, and if she didn't, you knew that as well. All that time, Ethel had thought she had kept her secret, only to realize now that Brandy had known all along, but to Brandy, it never had been a big deal. Brandy liked people for who they were, not their color, race, or background. It was rare to find someone who could love and trust so openly but still be as hard as nails if she thought someone, including herself, was being wronged.

The birds tried to swerve at the last minute, veering off in opposite directions, but for those in the middle of the flock, it was too late to change direction, and they came crashing into the front windows. Everyone turned to shield his or her face from the inevitable explosion of glass, but the glass held as bird after bird slammed against it. The sound of wings was deafening, the squawks seemed endless, and the smacking sound the birds made when they hit the glass was unnerving. Then, as quickly as it had started, the commotion ended. The group watched in disbelief as the birds regrouped and flew off into the distant sky just as the last of the daylight dipped beyond the horizon.

"What the bloody hell just happened?" asked Mary, breaking the silence. She was half bent over behind the couch. "Still think it's my mind playing tricks?" she asked Hoffman.

Hoffman was at a loss for words. He stood there with an emotionless face.

"It was the salt line that made them veer off," said Benjamin. "If not for that, I think we would have had a very bad night."

"Fuck me!" said Shawn to no one in particular.

"He is already stronger than I thought," Phillip said, still gazing out the window.

"Look, I don't think it's safe for anyone to leave tonight. That thing is out there, and it may be waiting for one of us to come venturing out," Benjamin told the group. With that, he walked over to Mary, who was still shaking, and put his arm around her.

Phillip heard a sound and looked up to see Joe peeking out of the bedroom upstairs that Phillip had claimed for himself that morning. "It's all right, Joe. It's over. You can come down now."

Joe entered the hall timidly. It was hard to tell if he was still afraid or was ashamed at being caught hiding upstairs.

"Well then, I, for one, am staying," said Josette. "You couldn't get me outside that door alone now if you held a gun to my head."

"Me as well," said Mary. "You don't have to hit me in the head with a hammer to get me to believe in this monster of yours now."

"Well, as kind as your offer is, I am sorry, but I will be returning to my own place tonight," said Hoffman. "I will be back in the morning. We are still doing the investigation, are we not?"

"Yes," said Josette without a moment's hesitation. "Now more than ever, I must see that house." She turned to Benjamin for acknowledgment.

"I agree," Benjamin said.

Phillip and Franky looked at each other. They both knew she was right; their situation had turned into a quest for survival. Regardless of how hard they'd tried to avoid walking into the fire, the flames were once again at their feet.

"Well then, I want to be on my way. I have a lot to get done," said Hoffman.

"Don't be a fool, Tim. Stay here. There is more

than enough room," said Benjamin with a tone of concern in his voice.

"No, thank you kindly, but I belong at home." With that, he took up his coat and hat and made his way toward the door. "Don't worry. I will be careful, and I will see you all first thing in the morning."

After he left, there was an odd silence around the room. One could still see patches of blood and black pinfeathers stuck to the windows. For an extended time, the entire group simply looked silently out the windows into the darkness and then from one to another in disbelief at what had occurred.

"I hope Hoffman makes it home okay," Josette said, finally breaking the awkward silence.

"I am sure he will be fine," Phillip replied, realizing he had been holding her close to him the whole time. He no longer cared what the other group members thought; he wanted to make sure she was safe.

"So who's ready for a drink?" joked Benjamin.

"Make mine a double," said Franky.

CHAPTER 8

THE INVESTIGATION

Hoffman was good to his word and came knocking on the door just before sunrise. Unfortunately, no one in the flat was yet awake. Franky, who had spent the night sleeping on the sofa in the living room when he'd discovered Phillip and Josette heading together to the room next to his, woke and let him in.

"Good morning, Professor Lake. I hope you slept well last night," said a perky Hoffman, making his way through the door.

"Sh! Everyone is still sleeping." Franky was standing there in his tighty-whities with his morning wood prevalent and one eye barely open, scratching his distraught red head of hair.

"Good God, cover up, man. What did you all do—have a party after I left?"

"Something like that, I guess you might say," Franky replied just above a whisper.

"Really, well, we don't have all day to lollygag around, now, do we?" Hoffman said loudly.

Just then, the door to Benjamin's bedroom opened, and out he came in his silk robe and slippers. Yawning, he walked past both of them, offered a "Morning," and went to the coffeepot. Franky returned to the living room, grabbed his clothes off the floor, and made his way to the bathroom.

"So you did a little drinking last night, I see," said Hoffman with stiff judgment in his tone.

"Yes, we had some fun last night. You remember fun, don't you?"

"I was hoping to get an early start this morning," huffed Hoffman, sitting down at the kitchen table.

"We will. Look. Here comes Josette now, and Phillip is right behind her," said Benjamin, giving them both a funny look.

"Good morning," said Phillip, descending the stairs.

Hoffman and Benjamin wished him good morning in return.

Hoffman, oblivious to the situation, continued. "You know how bad traffic gets at this time of day, and you said we could only do this in daylight hours."

"For God's sake, Tim, we will get there when we get there," replied Benjamin, scooping coffee into the pot. "Please just let me have one cup before you start your nagging."

"Thought all you Irishmen drank tea, not coffee," said Phillip sarcastically.

"Really, cowboy? You want to go there this early in the morning?" replied Benjamin with half a grin.

Coming out of the bathroom, Franky ran into Josette and gave a large smile. She knew he knew she had spent the night with Phillip. Being the gentleman he was, though, he did not make any comments. Her face was a little flushed as she passed into the bathroom and closed the door.

Shawn too appeared at his bedroom door, yawning. Slowly, he started making his way down the stairs as well.

"Where is Joe? Did he stay last night?"

"I think he is still sleeping. There was a lot of snoring coming from his room last night. The man is so loud. I mean real loud," said Shawn.

Just then, Benjamin's bedroom door opened again, only this time, it was Mary who emerged, dressed in one of Benjamin's silk robes. She had the look of a kid getting caught with her hand in the cookie jar. With all the men looking at her, she made her way toward the bathroom.

"Josette is in that one," said Benjamin, adding water to the coffee maker.

"Thanks. I will just use the one upstairs," she said, turning and taking the stairs.

Everyone could see the look of disdain on Hoffman's face. "Well, I see you added our young Mary to your list of conquests," he said. "I guess she knows about the long line of other young ladies she has followed into your lair."

"Actually, she didn't ask," responded Benjamin, grabbing the morning paper from outside the front door and having a seat at the table.

"What about the long line of young men? Does she know about them as well?" Hoffman asked with a reddening face. They could all see how badly he wanted that one to sting.

"Nope, didn't ask about them either," responded the unshaken Benjamin, never looking up from his paper.

Now Hoffman did not even try to hide his anger. "Who's next? Ms. Josette?"

Phillip gave him a stern look. He was getting close to crossing the line.

"Or maybe Professor Lake is more to your liking."

Without looking up, Benjamin nonchalantly replied, "Well, he does have the best-looking ass here."

Shawn's fist hit the table hard. "Okay, I am sick of this kind of talk," he said. "I will not stand here and listen to this bullshit anymore."

Everyone looked shocked. Even Benjamin put down his paper and looked at Shawn, and for just a moment, a smile appeared on Hoffman's face.

Shawn turned and rubbed his ass suggestively through his pajamas. "My ass is a lot hotter than Franky's."

Everyone at the table, with the exception of Hoffman, burst out laughing. He, on the other hand, gave a loud grunt and walked out of the kitchen and up the stairs to wake Joe.

When the laughter died down, Phillip turned to the group. "Look, we need to take it a little easy on him. We still need to make it through the day."

"He had that one coming," said Shawn.

"No, Phillip's right," said Benjamin reluctantly. "I only have one more day in my life with him in it. Let's not poke the bear. Trust me, it was not my intention to have him discover Mary coming out of my bedroom. He is her boss after all."

"How is it he knows so much about your personal life anyway?" asked Shawn as he took a seat across from Benjamin at the table.

"He knows nothing; all he knows is what has been in the tabs. I only wish my life was that exciting. About a year ago, one of my staff—an upstairs maid, to be precise—went to the tabloids about my outrageous behavior. She neglected to tell them I had fired her a week before for stealing and had tried to get her help for her drug problem, one I fear she may never overcome. Anyway, she told the press stories of endless orgies at the estate and how I play on both sides of the fence, as it were. The truth is, I have never been involved in an orgy, let alone held one at my house. I do not, in fact, fancy men, though I would find nothing wrong with it if I did, and I don't believe it would be anyone's business if I did. In regard to the long line of females Tim spoke of, I have had an unimpressive record of three lovers over the past three years, with Mary being the third. If that makes me a sex machine, then I say oil me up, and let's party."

"Have you gone to the press to tell them the truth?" ask Franky.

"No, and I have no intentions of doing so. Frankly, I don't give a damn what people like Tim think about me. Being born into money makes you a target; someone will always hold it against you. I funded Tim's projects at first because I believed in him; he is good at what he does. But as far as the man himself, I no longer have any use for him; he judges others as if he has the moral or ethical standards to do so. Still, I do not wish him any ill will. After today, I hope he has whatever success he can find."

"But the girl—don't you want to get back at her for what she's done?" asked Shawn.

"That poor girl already has a life that sucks.

Why would I possibly want to make it worse? If anything, I hope she takes what money she received and gets help, though I strongly doubt she will. Besides, my getting involved would also keep my name out there. The tabs are ruthless; the best thing to do is to stay as far away from them as possible."

"Coffee is ready," said Phillip.

"Thank God!" Benjamin exclaimed. "Maybe now I can deal with all this shit."

By noon, all had arrived at Banthom House. As Josette exited the car and approached the house, she looked confused, as if something else were drawing her. As the others exited their assigned vehicles and walked toward the front door, she instead left the group and started down the brick walkway that led to the back of the house. Everyone stopped and watched, as she seemed to be in another world. Phillip had seen that look before in the dungeon and knew she was feeling or seeing something hidden from the rest of them.

"Now what?" exclaimed Hoffman, holding a large coffee cup with one hand and putting the key to the lock with the other.

Everyone ignored Hoffman and followed Josette. As they circled the house, the backyard opened up to a large plot of garden with rosebushes long dead from neglect and lonely flower beds filled with dried weeds. In the back of the yard, where the rock wall still stood, a storage shed stood next to a large pile of stones that had long been overgrown. Looking at the stone wall, everyone could see a large section was gone, as if it had collapsed inward and landed in one large heap. Next to the heap was a cellar door angled slightly into a man-made mound of sod and earth.

"That's a World War II bomb shelter," said Benjamin, pointing to the door.

"But Ireland was neutral during the war. Why a shelter?" said Franky.

"Actually, Dublin and nearby areas were bombed a total of seven times during the war, though Germany claimed the bombings were accidental," Benjamin said. "Many feared there would be another blitz here, so they built shelters."

Josette never paused; she continued her march straight to the cellar door. "He was buried there," she said, pointing to the pile of rocks on her right. "They took the mahogany door from the front of his house, placed him in the hole alive, and then lowered the door on top of him. Then they all took stones from his wall there and dropped them in one at a time on top of the door. I can hear his bones cracking over his screaming as the pile gets higher."

Everyone stared at Josette. She seemed dazed and had a faraway look in her eyes.

"Those kids could never have dug through those rocks and then replaced them," Hoffman said.

"They didn't," said Josette, and she opened the squeaking cellar door.

"Wait," said Shawn. "I need to go down first to get a shot of everyone descending."

The air coming from below was foul, and everyone took a step back. Shawn had just reached the bottom, when Josette and the others started down the ladder, lit only by the light of Shawn's camera. As if she had done it a thousand times, Josette reached above her head for a string, and at once, light came to the darkness. As she descended, the others looked at each other for assurance. Then Phillip walked up and followed her down. They all followed. At the bottom, the space was just wide enough to hold them all. It was completely bare except for empty shelving on the left wall.

"They did not dig through the stone, Dr. Hoffman, but under it," said Josette, pointing to a large hole dug into the side of the right wall. Two shovels lay on the floor in front of the opening.

"This proves nothing," snapped Hoffman.

"You're wrong," Phillip said. He reached into the gaping hole and pulled out a small piece of decayed wood that crumbled in his hands. As he was showing it to the group, stones started cascading out and landed at his feet.

"I gotta get out of here!" screamed Mary as she pushed her way to the ladder. Benjamin helped her up and then followed.

"This is all very interesting, but can we now get to investigating the house?" said Hoffman with disdain in his voice. He was obviously annoyed with the delay and was not buying any of this.

"Yes, I need to see the house now," responded Josette, taking no notice of Hoffman's tone.

Mary and Benjamin had made their way back to the cars before the rest had even started emerging from the shelter. Mary had been on a dead run the entire way with Benjamin in hot pursuit, so by the time they stopped, they were both winded. "I don't know why, Ben, but I have the strangest feeling that fucker is still here, waiting for us to go into the house. I just don't think I can do this."

"Mary, you don't have to go in," said Benjamin, trying to reassure her.

"Hoffman will want his fucking notes," she replied. "I just don't think I can do it. All of this is hitting me. I mean, when this all started, I thought it was a joke, but now, after the birds and after that pit of hell, I just don't think I can do this."

Benjamin grabbed her and held her close.

"Look, screw Hoffman. You don't have to do anything you don't want to. I know this is a lot to take in. Shit, I am scared out of my mind as well."

"Then let's just get the hell away from here, both of us. Let's just leave and never look back."

Benjamin saw tears building up behind Mary's sweet, gentle eyes. "He knows who we are. No matter what, he will be looking for us. We are a threat to him, and he knows it. If we do not put an end to him now before he finds one of the books, then we will not be able to stop it, and he will eventually come after all of us."

Mary took a deep breath and wiped the wetness from her face. "Yes, I know you're right, but I have a feeling this is not going to end well for some of us. He will not go down without a fight."

"Mary, if you want to walk away now, I don't blame you. Leave, and we will take care of him. It is my duty to fight, not yours. If you want out now, I will tell Hoffman myself."

"No, no, that's all right. I am feeling a little better now," she said unconvincingly. "I still don't know if I can go into that house, though."

Just then, the rest of the group started circling the house with Hoffman in the lead. "Josette, anything you are feeling, just state it out loud so Mary can take notes, and we will compile the notes later with the footage."

Benjamin gave Mary a smile. "Just say the word," he whispered.

Mary pondered for a moment. "Fuck it. I'm going in. If it's a fight, then it's a fight, and I, for one, will do my part."

Phillip walked up to the two and, looking at Mary, asked, "You okay?"

"She'll be fine," answered Benjamin for her.

Hoffman unlocked the front door, and everyone went inside. The last to enter was Mary, who was holding tightly to Benjamin with one hand and clutching her notepad in the other.

Shawn went to work at once on the equipment. There were hours of footage to go over. The cameras needed reloaded, and batteries needed replaced. Joe immediately went to work on the audio; surely there'd been a number of bumps in the night they would need to evaluate. As for Josette, she started walking from room to room—first upstairs and then downstairs, first front and then back—over and over again. Finally, when she reached the kitchen, she grabbed Benjamin lightly by the arm. "This house is clean," she whispered. "A house this old should have any number of spirits, and with the rituals that took place here—"

Benjamin offered her a smile.

"You had this house blessed, didn't you?" Josette asked as if she already knew the answer.

"Of course I did—the day I bought it. But I sure as hell wasn't going to tell Tim that," he responded.

"I have to see the pantry where they found the two children. I think that is the only place I will have contact."

"It's right behind you, behind that door," said Benjamin, pointing to a thin wooden door with an old-fashioned latch.

Phillip joined the two as he saw them making their way to the door. "Is that where they found the kids?" he asked.

"Yes," Benjamin responded just above a whisper, nodding in the direction of Hoffman, who was across the living room while taking readings, holding an electromagnetic reading device in one hand and a thermometer in the other. It was clear they did not want him included in the endeavor.

As Josette put her hands on the door, she took a deep breath. "They are still here," she said, and after taking another long, deep breath, she opened the door.

To Benjamin and Phillip, there was only an empty room, but to Josette, it was not empty at all. Sitting in the fetal position on the floor was the young girl who had been brutally murdered at the hands of Banthom. Her hair was matted and still stained with blood. Next to her stood her brother. His complexion was a horrific blue, and his eyes were sunken into his skull. It was he who spoke to her first. "I am not going to leave her. He has part of her we need back. I will not leave; she would be all alone."

"I know, baby," responded Josette.

Benjamin and Phillip looked in wonderment as Josette started talking to the open air. They both knew someone was there with them, even if they could not see.

Josette, being the professional she was, at once said, "They are both here, the boy and the girl. The boy is communicating, but the girl is still hiding her head." Josette knelt down on the floor to get closer to the girl's level. "Who did this to you, honey?"

Again, the boy answered. "She will not answer; she is afraid of him. It was a monster that killed us. We only want to move on, but he keeps her here."

Josette suddenly noticed the large gash running the length of his throat. "Where is this monster now, sweetie?" she asked the boy directly.

The boy shook his head back and forth. "You will need to ask the others. They know."

"What others? Where are they?" Josette asked.

Benjamin and Phillip listened to one side of a conversation and watched Josette stand and walk out the door with her arm extended as if she were holding the hand of a child. Shawn, Franky, and Dr. Hoffman saw her walk by with Phillip and Benjamin close behind; quietly, they followed.

"Shit," said Joe, holding a handheld device. "The temperature just dropped ten degrees."

Josette stopped at the front door and bent down. "The boy wants to tell me something," she said to the group. The boy looked directly into her eyes and then pointed toward the front of the house. "I'm confused, sweetie. Are they outside?" Josette looked out one of the front windows. "He is just pointing toward the front door."

"Ask them to move something. The table, the chair—anything so we can get it on film," said Hoffman loudly. "Shawn, are you getting this? What am I paying you for?"

"I have gotten every moment since she walked out of the pantry," Shawn huffed.

The boy did not seem to hear anyone else in the room but Josette. He walked to the window, stood by her, and pointed again, this time directly out the window. "Now he is pointing out the front window," she said, and then she said to the boy, "I still don't understand. Can you tell me where they are?"

The boy did not say a word; he just pointed.

"Are you afraid he will come for you if you help us?" asked Josette.

"Ask him to show himself for the camera. Damn, woman, we need to get this on film," Hoffman said.

"Shut the fuck up," said Franky. "We need answers first."

Josette once again stared out the window. From upon the hill, she could see all the way down to the shore and beyond out to sea, and in the distance was Dalkey Island. "Are they out on the island? Is that where we need to go?"

The boy nodded.

"What island are they talking about?" Phillip whispered to Benjamin.

"It has to be Dalkey Island," he responded.

"The boy nodded in agreement. We need to go out to that island. There are more spirits out there," Josette told the others.

"Bullshit. If you are talking to the boy right now, ask him how his sister died." Hoffman spoke in a sarcastic tone.

This time, the boy did not ignore him; he turned and gave him a hateful glare. Then he was gone.

"You made him leave," said Josette.

Without warning, the coffee mug Hoffman had carried in with him that morning and set on the windowsill went flying across the room and struck him straight in the groin. He at once doubled over in pain.

"I got it," said Shawn, looking up from the camera.

For the next four hours, they continued the

investigation, but Josette made no further contact. There were no hidden secrets in the house. The boy and girl would not appear again, no matter how much Josette pleaded. Phillip finally insisted they call it a day and said the island was the place they needed to be; his faith in Josette was complete. If she said the boy had pointed them there, then that was where they should be. Over Hoffman's continued reluctance, Benjamin, Phillip, Franky, Josette, and Shawn set off for the island. At first, Hoffman insisted Shawn stay to help with the equipment, but Benjamin gave Hoffman a glimmer of hope that they might come back to do a nighttime follow-up investigation when he said, "Leave it. I have a feeling we are not done here yet. Don't worry. I will pay the additional cost."

"I would like to leave as well if that is okay," said Mary. "I need to type up these notes, and I am so very tired."

"Fine," said Hoffman.

Chapter 9

DALKEY ISLAND

It was early evening by the time the ferry left Coliemore Harbour and arrived on the island. Benjamin was the only one who had ever been to the island before; he knew there was not much to see. Luckily, it was late enough in the day that most of the tourists had left for the day, and the anglers had all gone home. The air was cool but not cold; a steady breeze came from the east. If they'd not been on such a dangerous venture, thought Benjamin, it would have been a pleasant early evening.

As they passed the remains of the old seventh-century church, Josette gave a long sigh. "I know he has been here. I feel it."

"All I feel is the pain in my legs. All we are doing is going uphill!" said Phillip, sounding winded.

"I don't get it. If salt keeps him from coming

through doors, how does he get to an island surrounded by salt water?" Shawn asked Franky.

"I don't know. Maybe he brought a boat. There are plenty around here for him to choose from, or maybe the water dilutes the salt so it has no effect. If so, he could swim."

"The salt must be pure," said Benjamin, who'd overheard the conversation. "I would speculate that salt water would not bother him."

"Sorry to keep being such a bother with the questions," Shawn said, "but how did the kids know he was even there to be unearthed? I mean, surely they did not know the story of Banthom."

"I can answer that one," Phillip said. "I had a very dear friend named Kip Gillmore. You heard me talk about him last night at the table. When we were kids, he actually heard the witch Fritz pleading with him from the grave to release him. I think if someone is young and sensitive enough, he or she can be manipulated by a witch, even from six feet under. There is little doubt the same kids in Michigan whom Fritz slaughtered by his grave released him in the first place. He willed them to dig him up. The same thing happened here."

"Remember, they do not die; they just lie in wait," added Franky.

As they approached the Martello Tower, a large lookout tower from days gone by, goats, which none of them had seen before that, came rushing up from behind, giving them all a start.

"I guess we are all a little jumpy," Shawn said to Franky.

In the distance, they could see a lighthouse perched on a lifeless island of rock.

"That place—there is something there. I can feel it," Josette said.

"Now, hold on," said Benjamin. "There's no ferry going out to that island."

"We don't need to go to that island. They are coming here." Only Josette could see the six ghostly figures floating above the water while slowly and methodically making their way to Dalkey Island. Josette felt drawn to them. She felt them summoning her forward, and slowly, she made her way toward the eastern shore to meet them.

"What do you think she sees?" Benjamin asked Phillip.

"Knowing her, the question is who, not what," responded Phillip.

"There are three women, two men, and one small girl. They all look as if their midsections have been torn away. I can see right through them," Josette said as she walked.

Franky wanted desperately to ask, "Can you see through the apparitions or just their midsections?" but he held his tongue.

"They are all so decomposed, just like the little girl back at the house. The boy wasn't that gruesome. I wonder why," Josette said, speaking more to herself than anyone in the group.

"Josette!" yelled Phillip, grabbing her just before she walked over the edge of the grass onto the rocks below.

"They are trying to kill you!" exclaimed Benjamin.

"No, they are not trying to hurt me. They are pointing down to the rocks below. There is something there they want me to see."

"Now, wait a minute. I don't know that this is such a good idea," said Phillip.

"Help me down, will you, Franky?" she said, ignoring Phillip.

Franky gave a look Phillip's way, and not getting any resistance, he slowly descended to the first pile of rocks and then held his arms out to assist Josette. Phillip, Benjamin, and Shawn followed suit. The rocks were tricky, to say the least; they all took their time in making sure they had solid footing before the next step.

Halfway down, Josette stopped. "It's here. Right here—" Before she could finish her sentence, she saw standing on the last few feet of stone before the water's edge a large black cat. Its back was hunched, its ears were all the way back, and it was showing its teeth and hissing. Without warning, it leaped directly at Josette and knocked her backward. She landed roughly on her backside. A swift kick from Benjamin's boot sent the cat smashing into the large boulder where Franky was perched. It fell limply at his feet. Franky, without thinking twice, picked up a large stone and brought it down hard on the cat's head. As the rock made its impact, the body of twelve-year-old Annie Nash sat up from behind a crevasse in the rocks near were Josette sat and grabbed her arm. None had seen her there just moments before.

"He lied!" screamed Annie, staring blankly at Josette.

Josette's entire body started to shake, and then she let out an ear-piercing scream of pain.

Phillip rushed over and tried to pry the girl's grip from Josette's arm, but it was like a vise. Then, suddenly, Annie Nash's body went limp, her hand let go, and she fell lifelessly back into the crevasse of rocks.

To the amazement of all, the cat stood once again, its disfigured head teetering on its fractured neck. Laughter emerged, deep and sinister, from behind the cat's broken teeth. It was Franky who kicked it this time, out into the open water, where it silently sank below the waves. All attention now turned back to Josette, who was in the fetal position, weeping uncontrollably.

Phillip went to her and held her tightly in his arms.

"My God, I felt them both, the girl and Banthom all at once," she managed to say.

"Are you okay?" asked Phillip with sympathy in his voice. He reached down to help her up, but she pushed him away.

"Give her a minute," said Franky. "She looks like she is in shock."

The group stood there for a good ten minutes, waiting for some sign from Josette. Finally, she looked up at them and said, "That foul creature was in my head. I could hear him speak. I could see his thoughts." Then, slowly, she got up, still shaking. A large red hand mark was on her wrist. "He is leaving Dublin," she said.

Thinking back on earlier that day, Joe recalled that Mary had been the last to leave with all her notes in tow. She obviously had been in a hurry to part ways with the house. Joe had waved goodbye to her through the front window of Banthom House as she got in her car; if only she knew she was already his. The others had just departed for their island adventure, and Joe knew what they would find there, but it did not matter. If things went as planned, he would not be seeing any of them for quite a while. Hoffman had promised they would be off the premises by dark, but Joe knew he could keep Hoffman looking at the video for as long as he needed, and now, with the sun sinking over the hilltop, he knew it would not take long. He was not nervous—not as much as he'd thought he would be anyway—for the events to unfold. After all, Mary would be his when all was said and done. "You really need to see this next tape, Dr. Hoffman. I think I saw an orb about halfway through. It was as clear as you can get," he said, handing the video to the doctor. "I will finish with the cabling while you give it a once-over."

Hoffman had had enough. "Joe, I am ready to go. I promised we would be off the premises by dark."

"But, Professor Hoffman, I still have some stuff to load. Why don't you just review this next tape once more before we leave?"

Hoffman thought for a moment. "No, I gave my word. I will help you with the last bit, and then let's get out of here. Look—it's already getting dark."

Joe hesitated for just a moment and then said, "You're the boss. Can you hand me that hammer in my tool bag over there? I stapled some cabling along the stairway, and I need to pry it lose."

Hoffman walked over to the large black satchel on the floor, retrieved the hammer, and walked toward Joe with a puzzled look on his face. "You didn't staple any cabling."

Joe's patience was running out with the old man. "Just give me the fucking hammer."

"Now, wait a minute. Just who in the hell do you think you are, talking to me that way?"

In one single motion, Joe reached out, grabbed the hammer from Hoffman's still outstretched hand, and swung with all his might, digging the tooth edge straight into Hoffman's right knee. Hoffman at once went to the ground, grabbing his leg in pain. Without stopping, Joe walked around him and repeated the blow, this time to his left knee. Hoffman, in shock, could only look up at Joe in disbelief.

"You always have to do things the hard way," said Joe. "You old fucking—"

Joe was stopped short by a pair of headlights pulling up the drive. He ran to the window and saw a car he had never seen before pull up. A stranger, a huge man, got out of the car first, giving him a fright, but then came the dark figure he had been waiting for. It was time. Joe had finished loading the equipment hours ago, but upon arrival, his van had been filled with more than just equipment. While Hoffman had been busy with the videos, Joe had been busy taking supplies out of his van and loading Hoffman's car.

"Why are you doing this?" Hoffman said.

"Shut up, you old fool! You wanted proof of the afterlife. Well, fucker, here it comes."

Through the doorway walked the dark figure of Banthom, his face hidden by the shadows. Joe could hear him sniffing the air like someone waiting for a Thanksgiving feast. The creature fell to the floor and scurried over to Hoffman on all fours, more like a spider than any human. Though Hoffman screamed as loud and long as he could, it made no difference; within seconds, Banthom was on him, feeding. Joe had to turn his head from the onslaught, but still, he could hear Hoffman's screams joined with the sound of Banthom's ripping teeth.

The ride back to Benjamin's flat was quiet; Josette had not uttered a word since her revelation that Banthom was leaving. Phillip checked her arm, which was still red and bruised from the girl's tense grip. Everyone had agreed that once they returned to Benjamin's abode, they would give an anonymous tip regarding the whereabouts of the bodies. The last thing they needed at that point was to be caught up in an extended investigation, especially now that they knew Banthom was on the move. Even with everything that had already taken place, Benjamin and Shawn both seemed in a state of shock.

Franky sympathized with them. This was not his first rodeo with dead creatures coming back to life, and he had the feeling it might not be his last. He remembered the terror he'd felt when confronted with pure evil for the first time. Phillip gave him a look of "I know what you are thinking" from the backseat, where he held tightly to a still-motionless Josette. The hard part was coming up with anything to say to try to ease their troubled minds.

"We need to warn Hoffman," Shawn said. "He may not believe it, but he is in danger like the rest of us."

"I will call him when we get back to my flat," Benjamin said, "but I doubt it will do any good. Besides, Josette said he was leaving."

"That doesn't mean he won't do some damage before he goes," responded Shawn.

"Point well taken, but first, I think we need to take her," Benjamin said, nodding toward Josette, "to the hospital. She needs to be looked at."

"No," Josette said softly from the backseat, where she still had her face buried in Phillip's chest. "I am not going to any hospital. Trust me. They cannot help me with this."

"Josette said five, so he is not as far along as we thought," Phillip said to Franky.

"Six," Shawn said. "Three women, two men, and a little girl."

"He will still need more to be whole," Phillip said. "Fritz was close, but six did not do it for him.

If Banthom was truly crushed by stones, God only knows how many more it may take to make him human again."

"Benjamin, can we use your influence in town to help track him down? We need to know where he is going," Franky said.

"A blue boat. He is leaving in a blue sailboat," responded Josette.

Mathew Duryee's mind raced as he drove along the back roads in Hoffman's car. He'd been more than glad to shed his getaway car, broken back window and all. The thought of what he had just seen lay heavily on his mind; he couldn't believe the savagery that had taken place. He had seen a man ripped apart in a matter of minutes.

Is any of this real? Mathew thought to himself. It all seemed like some kind of drug-induced dream from which he could not awaken. The creature sleeping beneath the blankets in the backseat stirred, and Mathew got a cold chill down his spine. It was covered now from head to foot, but its presence was just as strong. It felt as if he were sitting in the seat next to Mathew, watching. One touch—that was all it had taken. With one touch, he had gone from near death to feeling stronger than he had ever felt in his life. The creature had assured him that as easily as he had healed him, he could return him to his former state. Mathew had no doubt in his mind that the creature spoke the truth. The night before, when Banthom had left him alone in an old, abandoned house in Dalkey, he'd thought long and hard about fleeing, and even now, he had brief impulses to simply stop the car and run away as fast as he could into the darkness, but he knew that if he left, it would be his end. There was no hiding from the thing. It knew his thoughts and his every move. Money, sex, power, and immortality—those were the things it had promised, and they would only cost him his mortal soul. Mathew knew the time to prove his loyalty was at hand; he would need to complete the ritual. "That which binds us to him," the creature had told him. Mathew did not know what to expect, but he knew he would regret it.

"Thanks, Joe. Have a good evening," said Benjamin into the phone. After several attempts at calling Hoffman, Benjamin had given up and called Joe to see if he knew where he was. Phillip, who'd just left the upstairs bedroom, came into the kitchen, where Benjamin and Shawn stood. "She is out like a light," he said in reference to Josette.

"I have been trying to get ahold of Hoffman. I finally called Joe, but he said he hasn't seen Hoffman since he left the house," Benjamin told

Phillip and Shawn. "He said Hoffman was still loading equipment when he left."

"That's odd," responded Shawn. "Hoffman's brainless when it comes to technology. He knows what it all does, but he doesn't have clue how to set it up or tear it down, and I've never seen him lift anything more than his notepad. I can't believe he would let Joe go before everything was torn down and loaded. Joe even had to convince him he could do it all himself before he gave in to my going with you."

"What about Mary? Did you try calling her? She may know where he is," Phillip said.

"She's getting changed in my bedroom. She arrived right after you went upstairs with Josette. She said she left the two not long after we left for the island."

"You don't think he is trying to do a nighttime investigation himself, do you?" asked Phillip. "You know how hot on the idea he was."

"Not without Joe and me there. He would want it documented. Trust me. That's what he is all about—showing proof," responded Shawn before Benjamin could answer. "I'm telling you. Something is not right about all of this."

Benjamin reluctantly said, "We need to go back to the house if there's a chance—"

"God, I wish you hadn't said that," responded Shawn. "Besides, maybe he is just out for dinner, or maybe he went to have a drink to celebrate his achievement of getting into the house." Shawn spoke in such a tone that all could tell he himself did not believe it. Both men gave him looks. "Fine. I'll go."

"Do you think Mary will be good enough to stay with Josette?" Phillip asked Benjamin. "She is in rough shape. There is no way she can make this trip."

"Has she said anything else?" asked Benjamin.

"Vague references to the cat and girl being connected somehow, and she says she made a momentary connection with Banthom. Said she had never felt such evil."

"Any more about him leaving?" asked Shawn hopefully.

"All she will say is he is leaving in a big blue sailboat."

At that moment, a loud knock on the door made all three grown men jump.

CHAPTER 10

A FOND FAREWELL

Twelve-year-old Tyler Boland sat awake in his bedroom, staring out into the dim light offered by the streetlamps. He hated the new house in the city. Why had his mom married that person anyway? He missed his friends in Portrane; he missed their little two-bedroom house; and most of all, he missed sharing a room with his sister, Lilly. Since moving in, he'd been frightened to death of sleeping alone, with all the noise of cars passing by, people talking as they walked along the sidewalk below his bedroom window, and dogs barking. He wanted out of the city and back where he felt safe.

Tyler got out of bed and walked over to open his bedroom door. His new dad was away on business for the next two nights, so at least he didn't have to worry about sleeping with his door open, something he was not allowed to do when his stepfather was at home. "Stop being such a baby," he would say. "Grow up and be a man." That night, like most nights, Tyler got up and opened it anyway; he had learned how to open it in stealth mode without making a sound. Lilly, always the first up in the family, would close it when she got up to make sure he did not get in any trouble. She was the greatest.

As he opened the door, he saw in the pale light a dark figure slinking into his mom's bedroom. At first, he thought it a trick of the eyes, but as he watched through the open door, he saw it again, moving toward his mom's bed. Fright overtook him as he hid behind his half-open door, frozen, unable to move or speak. Then came the sound of footsteps on the stairs. Maybe his new dad had come home early. *Please let it be my new dad!* Before the man's head had even cleared the top step, Tyler knew that was not the case. Even with the limited light, it was clear the man had a head full of hair, and his new dad shaved his head. Quickly, Tyler took a step back into his room and slowly closed his door to a crack so that he could see without being seen. Rather than turning left into his mom's bedroom, the new intruder turned left into Lilly's.

A burst of sound emanated from his mother's room. He could hear her screaming in fear, and he heard things breaking, as if his mother were fighting off the invader. Tyler could feel his heart pounding in his chest. He felt as if he were going to get sick. Backing up even more, he bumped into the mirrored sliding door of his closet, which was open. As deliberately and quietly as he could, he climbed in and sat down gently on the floor. From there, he knew he would not be able to see anything that was going on, but at that point, he didn't want to see. He reached up and closed the door behind him. Within a matter of minutes, the screaming stopped. *God, please let someone have heard and called for help*, he thought. No sooner had the screaming stopped than he heard his sister's muffled cries coming from her room, as if someone had his hands covering her mouth. Then came silence. Sitting in the darkness, he did not hear a sound other than his own heavy breathing. Though hiding only for a few minutes, to Tyler, it was an eternity. He felt faint, and he could not control the runaway thoughts going through his brain. *What did they do to Mom and Lilly? Did they kill them? Are they dead? For God's sake, are they dead?* Maybe he could help them, but how? Maybe he should run and try to get past them and down the stairs. Then he could run to the neighbors to get help. Then it happened: he heard the familiar squeak his bedroom door made when opening. He had spent a long time learning how to prevent that squeak. There was no doubt they were coming in; they were in his room. Heaven help him, they were in his room. Tyler feared his loud breathing would give him away and tried hard to slow it down, but it was no use. He heard footsteps just beyond the closet door. Slowly and as silently as he could, he inched his way deeper into the closet. Lucky for him, Tyler had a bad habit of throwing all his dirty clothes onto his closet floor rather than taking them the few extra steps to the bathroom hamper. He grabbed at the pile of dirty clothes, buried himself, and then curled into a ball as far away from the door as possible. Just as he was settled in, he heard his closet door slide slowly open. Tyler thought he could see through the T-shirt covering his face the shadow of a man's head pop into view. It appeared to look left and then right and then slowly retreat. Tyler heard the figure walk over to his bed and grunt as he bent down. *He must be looking under my bed*, thought Tyler. Then he heard the stranger walking toward the door and heard the familiar squeak as the door shut. Tyler allowed himself the luxury of a deep breath. In the darkness, he sat shaking and all alone. There was not a sound from anywhere in the house. Time seemed to stand still, but his racing mind did not. Maybe they were gone; maybe they had given up searching for him. His thoughts went to his mother and sister; he could picture them lying dead on their beds. He started to weep. How could this be happening? Had he heard them walk down the steps? Had he heard a sound from downstairs? His brain could no longer discern what was real. Then came thoughts of his own survival. How long should he wait until he bolted out of the house? Would they catch him if he did? How long could he stay in one spot, for God's sake? When would this end? A million emotions rushed over him all at once. That was when he felt the claw grabbing at him. In a flash, it had him and yanked him out of the closet with one swift motion. At arm's length, he looked directly into the bloodstained grin of the monster. It was cloaked in black, its face thin and pale. It looked as if someone had taken a sledgehammer to its skull, which was full of large dents with pieces of broken bone protruding in different directions. At that instant, another man came walking into his room. To the left of him was Lilly, standing in the doorway. She was staring straight ahead with a blank look upon her face, as if in trance, taking no notice of him, the stranger, or the beast that held him above its head with one arm. Tyler, still trying to take in his circumstances, started to violently kick and scream, trying to loosen the creature's grip.

"Look at me, boy!" demanded the beast.

Benjamin did not return to the flat until early the next morning. The night had been long and exhausting. Upon his arrival home, Franky and a still-distraught Josette were sitting at the kitchen table. Phillip and Shawn, who were in the living room watching the morning news, jumped up once they saw him come through the door and met him in the kitchen. At that point, all Benjamin wanted to do was go to bed, but he knew that before he did, he would need to retell his night's adventures to the group.

"So what did the police want?" asked Shawn, sitting down.

Benjamin ignored his request momentarily and walked over to pour himself a cup of coffee. Then he sat down at the kitchen table, gave a smile to Josette, and began. "Hoffman is dead; they found him at Banthom House about an hour before they came here."

They all let out loud gasps.

Benjamin continued. "It being my property, they wanted to know why he was at one of my residences. I had to tell them about the investigation and about everyone being there. I told them we had all left early, and the only ones left in the house were Joe and Hoffman. They sent a car to pick up Joe, but apparently, no one was at home. I told them we had just talked to him before they arrived at the door, but they waited all night, and he never showed."

"How did it happen? I mean, how did he die?" Phillip asked.

"They said Hoffman was found on the floor. Much like the girl from a few weeks ago, he was, it seemed, half eaten. Then they mentioned they had received an anonymous tip about a body on Dalkey Island and more at the lighthouse. They are going out there today to investigate to see if there is any connection."

"Do they think we had anything to do with his murder?" asked Phillip.

"Well, it seems the reason they stopped at the house to begin with was the car they saw in the driveway." Benjamin could see the bewilderment in everyone's face. "The car was stolen by a man they believe to be a paid assassin."

"This just keeps getting better and better," said Shawn.

"When they flashed their torches in the front window, there was Hoffman, laid out on the floor," Benjamin said. "For now, all the attention is on this stranger."

"Then what took so long? We were afraid they were putting you through some sort of interrogation," said Franky.

"They took me over to the house. I opened it, and they asked if anything was missing or out of place or if we had seen anything during our investigation. They collected all the evidence they could and asked if we had been doing any recording during the investigation and if they could get the film, and then they apologized for keeping me so long and brought me home."

"What did you tell them about the film?" asked Shawn, knowing his camera was still full of shots from the house and the island. The footage would be a dead giveaway they were the ones who'd called in the tips.

"I told them everything was in the back of Joe's van," Benjamin replied.

"Shit!" exclaimed Phillip. "It has been there all along." All the groups' attention turned to him. Once again, Phillip took on his take-charge tone they had all come to know. "Don't you see? Josette warned Benjamin and me that someone in the group would betray us."

"Joe!" said Franky. "It has to be Joe."

"Yes, I believe so," replied Phillip.

"The birds. Remember the birds?" said Shawn with excitement. "He went downstairs to the parking garage to get his camera and was down there for a long time. Then, the next thing we knew, we were attacked. Maybe he was down there letting this bastard know we were all here and that it was the time to strike, to kill all of us at once."

"And when they did arrive, he was upstairs—doing what?" asked Franky.

"Can't you see? Last night was not about killing anyone; it was a distraction. He went upstairs to retrieve my address book," replied Phillip. "Remember, it was gone the next morning. I accused you of leaving it at the hotel but then remembered I had looked up Hoffman's number after that."

"How could he possibly know about your book?" Franky said.

"I used the damn thing at Hoffman's the first day we got here to write down everyone's contact information. He knew I had it."

"But why?" asked Benjamin.

"The one question Banthom needed an answer to was where the other grimoires were. Now he knows," said Phillip, almost as an apology.

"How? I am still a little lost on all this," Benjamin said.

"Joe overheard me tell Josette that the book was safe with a friend in Florida. The only person from Florida I had in my black address book was the person we sent the book to."

"Oh my God, Mrs. Cartwright! He is on his way to Florida." Franky gasped. "But what about your sister? Doesn't she live in Florida?" he asked with a small glimmer of hope.

"No, she got a divorce more than a year ago. She lives in Boston now. I erased her old address and replaced it with her new one," replied Phillip.

The look on Benjamin's face said it all. "After all this time, the bastard will get his book back."

"Benjamin, I can't tell you how sorry I am about this. I never saw Joe eavesdropping. I thought the two of us were alone."

"No, Phillip, please don't blame yourself for this. He is a cleaver son of a bitch. I think he would have found it no matter what we did. It's my fault for not coming to you years ago and telling you the whole story. I guess I just never really thought any of this was real."

"I know that Banthom is leaving by boat. The girl told me when we had our connection. I don't know where, but if the book is indeed in Florida and he's going by boat, it will take him a long time to get there," Josette said timidly, taking everyone by surprise. That was the most she had spoken all morning.

"It makes sense. How else could you get a creature like that to the States, other than hiding it in the bottom of a boat?" Shawn said.

"Banthom is smart—a lot smarter than the witch we faced last time," said Phillip. "He hasn't been in any hurry. He's taken his time, killed slowly, and then hidden the bodies. He planned this all out and sought help from Joe and most likely this assassin character. He's building his forces as he goes. It makes sense he would travel by boat; he would not exactly blend in when boarding a plane."

"That does not mean he hasn't sent Joe ahead," Josette said.

Franky and Phillip looked at each other with the realization that Joe could be on a plane to Florida that minute. "Phillip, we've got to go, and we need to go now," said Franky.

Just as Franky was finishing his statement, Mary called from the living room, "All of you need to come hear this!" All of them rushed to where she stood staring at the television.

"Now, as promised, the continuation of this special report. Two children are missing from their home on St. Gabriel's Road after their mother was found murdered in what appears to be an animal attack. The brother and sister are ages—"

"That's near the docks," said Mary.

"He's starting to rebuild his cult. He's repeating the ritual," Phillip said.

Ethel was surprised when there came a loud knocking at her front door. Outside, she heard Brandy's voice through the door. "Ethel, you out of bed yet? I got a call from Franky and Phillip last night. They are on their way here, and we need to take this book and put it somewhere safe. Ethel get up. It's almost noon, for God's sake! Ethel!"

Ethel opened the door and looked down at the woman standing on the front steps. "Woman, are you out of your godforsaken mind? What the hell are you talking about?"

"We need to hide this fucking book; something evil is after this thing. I've got to get it out of my house and somewhere safe. Come with me to the bank."

"I am not going any fucking place until you slow down, come inside, and tell me what the hell is going on here. You understand me?" said Ethel.

"But—"

"But nothing! Now, get your fat old-lady ass up these steps, and come in for coffee. You need to let me know what is going on before I do anything."

Once inside, Brandy spilled the beans on everything she knew about the murders in Parksville, Michigan. She told Ethel about the evil presence in her house and about everything Franky had conveyed to her long ago regarding their fight with a witch. Then she told her about the call from Phillip and Franky late last night with word that they were flying to Florida. They'd warned her that someone else might beat them there in search of the package they had sent her, perhaps an Oriental man in his early twenties. They'd pleaded with her to make sure that whatever happened, he did not get his hands on it. They'd told her about a new witch, one more powerful and dangerous than the last. They had even begged her to leave and go somewhere safe.

Ethel listened to every word, waiting until Brandy was done to speak. Finally, she said, "And that package—it has the book?"

"Yes. I know it sounds crazy, but I swear it's all true."

Before Ethel could respond, they heard a car approaching. It appeared to be slowing down in front of their homes. Brandy got up and ran out the door with Ethel right behind her. The car had not pulled into either driveway but, rather, had stopped across the street. It was a little foreign car—a mini-something, thought Ethel. Behind the wheel was a man of Oriental descent. He was looking at Brandy strangely, as if he had bad intentions. He opened the door of the car to emerge.

"Shit!" exclaimed Brandy. Then, without a moment's hesitation, she hurriedly walked back into her house.

Ethel did not know what do. Should she follow, wait, confront the stranger, or go back to her television? It was obvious the stranger was the man Brandy's friends had warned her about. In less than a minute, Brandy reemerged with a phone in one hand and her shotgun in the other.

"Now that's what I'm talking about!" said Ethel, nodding her approval.

As soon as the man saw the shotgun, he shut his car door and quickly drove away.

"That man gave me the creeps. I will be glad when those friends of yours get here," Ethel said.

"You coming to the bank with me or not?" snapped Brandy.

"You know I am. Just let me lock up real quick," responded Ethel as she went in to grab her purse and keys.

Joe, shocked by the sight of the shotgun, had left but had not traveled far away. All day, he had worked on how he would approach the old woman to gain access to her house. He'd had the whole thing figured out. He'd just say he was looking for a home for his elderly mother and was asking the people there how they felt about the park so he could be sure he was making the right choice.

He had never expected to be looking down the barrel of a gun. That had been a surprise for sure. But as he thought it through, it became clear: Parker had already figured out he had betrayed them, and he had warned the old woman before Joe got there. He sat just behind the clubhouse in his parked car, training binoculars on the far reaches of the mobile home park. From there, he could see Brandy's trailer, and he watched as she and her neighbor got into a car. In her hand was a package covered in brown paper. Now he was faced with another choice: to break into the house while they were gone or follow them. If the old lady was afraid, maybe she would be inclined to get the book out of her house as soon as possible. If so, he would need to follow to see the package's destination. If not, he would lose a prime opportunity to search her home undetected. Was the package, his master prize, with them or did the book lay hidden in the old goat's bedroom? This was a dilemma he had not counted on. Making up his mind, he slowly followed the old women out of the park, staying far enough behind not to be seen.

CHAPTER 11

FLORIDA

Franky had not closed his eyes the entire trip. As they circled Tampa Bay, his anxiety rose even more. He knew he had to get to Mrs. Cartwright's as soon as possible.

"I wonder what it cost Benjamin to fly us here first class," Phillip said in a feeble attempt to wipe the look of concern off Franky's face.

"I'm sure it wasn't cheap," Franky replied. "But I am glad he got us here as quickly as he did, first class or not."

"Now, don't you worry about Brandy. If I know her, she is sitting on her front porch with that shotgun of hers laid across her lap," Phillip said with a grin.

Franky could not suppress a grin himself. "You know, I bet you're not far off with that one."

"From what Benjamin has told me, I figure it

will take about six weeks for them to sail from Dublin to Tampa," Phillip said.

"Yes, but Joe is already there," said Franky. "I swear, if he touches her, I will—"

"He won't. Trust me on this one. She is fine." Phillip spoke with a degree of certainty.

Somewhat reassured, Franky turned and looked out the window into the darkness. They would be at her door in less than an hour.

"It's beautiful, isn't it?" said Phillip, looking out the window. The bay was outlined with lights like a giant pearl necklace on the neck of an invisible goddess. It was huge, with three strings of lights running its length across. Upon their coming closer, the lights turned out to be bridges crossing the bay. "It's been years since I was here, man. I can't even remember my last visit."

Franky knew Phillip was talking about his trips to visit his sister, who once had lived in Clearwater. Though Phillip and his sister talked all the time on the phone, Franky knew it had been years since Phillip had been down to Florida. Now that her husband was out of the picture—he was a real asshole according to Phillip—maybe Phillip would visit her more often, this time in Boston, where she had moved. It was hard to say with Phillip; he liked his simple life. Above everything else, he loved to teach. Still, with Franky going to live in Ann Arbor, maybe Phillip would travel more and go see more people.

"Benjamin said he has a car waiting. I hope it's big enough for all of us," said Phillip.

"Knowing Benjamin, it's a limo," Franky joked.

"That would be awesome," replied Phillip. "I've never been in a limo."

Franky gave him another grin.

"I can't believe everyone agreed to come help, even Mary," said Phillip.

"Don't underestimate Mary; there is more to her than I think any of us realize."

"Phillip, will you come here a minute?" asked Benjamin from two rows back.

Phillip unbuckled his seat and got up, leaving Franky sitting alone.

For some strange reason, Franky's thoughts went to his mother. She would have loved it there in first class. He knew that even if she'd had the money, she would have still flown coach; she would never have wasted money on a first-class ticket. He could hear her telling him, "You can get there just the same in any seat on the plane." But a free ticket—she would have been in on that in a heartbeat. He smiled at the thought; they had known each other well. He still missed her so much. How many more mothers would die? How many more sons, daughters, and fathers? Franky knew if they did not kill Banthom soon, many more families would be torn apart.

"Damn, girl, you are going to wear a path in that carpet! They will be here when they get here," Ethel said to Brandy. "Stop pacing and wringing your hands. I know you're nervous, but now you're making me nervous too. Come sit down, and drink your tea."

Brandy slowly made her way to the table and sat down. "I cannot believe this is all happening again."

"I know I plan on giving Phillip and Franky a piece of my mind. That's what I know. Why in the hell they ever sent you that vile thing is beyond me. What were they thinking? Why did they have to bring you into this?"

Brandy smiled broadly. It was the first time Ethel had seen her smile since Phillip and Franky had called to tell her they were on their way and were bringing some friends with them. "Ethel, these men mean the world to me; they would never have put me in danger knowingly. They sent it to me because I am probably the only one in the world they could trust with something so important. Franky told me that Phillip was sure someone was invading their house, looking for the book. That thing can never fall into the wrong hands. Of that I am sure." Brandy reached over and took Ethel's hand in hers. "Whether I like it or not, I am a part of this, but you need to leave for a while. Go visit some family or something. This is not on you."

Ethel leaned over and looked Brandy straight in the eyes, and as she did so, the grip on her hand got more forceful. "You can kiss my black ass! I am not going nowhere. You hear me? If you think for one minute you are going to face all this without me, you are even more of a crazy old bitch than I thought."

Brandy smiled. She wanted Ethel to go but was glad she was staying. "You are one stubborn old goat."

Brandy at once recognized the voices of Phillip and Franky coming from outside the door. After putting the shotgun to one side, she walked to the door and opened it before they even had a chance to knock.

"Mrs. Cartwright, I am so glad to see you," said Franky, walking in and giving Brandy a huge hug.

"Oh, Franky, you look so grown up. How long has it been?"

Next came Phillip, who also gave her a big hug. "You look younger than ever," he said.

"Then I must have looked a thousand the last time you saw me," Brandy responded. She gestured toward Ethel. "This is Ethel, the one I have told you so much about."

"I am so pleased to meet you," said Phillip. "Brandy talks about you all the time."

"If it was anything bad, she's lying." Ethel smiled and shook his hand.

"And here is the rest of the crew," said Franky as, one by one, they made their way through the door. "This is Josette."

"Oh, I love that name," said Ethel.

"This is Benjamin, Shawn, and Mary."

"Oh, I am so glad to meet all of you. Please come in, and let me make everyone some tea or coffee, whichever you want," Brandy said excitedly.

"You just sit down and visit," said Ethel, getting up. "I'll take the orders, and you talk to these fine young people."

"I really need to use the loo, if you don't mind," said Josette.

"Me too," Mary said.

"I'll show you where it's at, honey. Right this way," said Ethel. As she turned to walk down the hall, she asked, "Coffee or tea?"

Josette and Mary answered at the same time, "Tea."

"You still have that thing, I see," said Phillip, pointing to the shotgun standing in the corner.

"Sorry. I need to put that away. A strange-looking Oriental man pulled up this morning. I don't know if it's the one you warned me about, but I do know he gave me the willies, and as soon as he saw Ethel come out the door, he pulled away," Brandy said, knowing all too well it was her shotgun that had scared him away, not Ethel.

Benjamin gave a look to the group, and they all knew what he was thinking.

"I got the bastard's plate number. Should I call the police?" Brandy said.

"Please, if you will give me the number, I will give it to the private eye I hired to help us. He should be here any minute. I hope you don't mind," replied Benjamin. "I don't think the police are the ones I need to call just now."

"Sure, not a problem, dear. Let me get my purse so I can give you the number."

"Thank you," said Benjamin.

"While I give this young man the number, the rest of you go sit down," said Brandy.

No sooner had Phillip sat down at the table than he asked in his right-to-the-point way, "Brandy, where is the book now?"

"Well, like I told you on the phone, it's safe. I put it where I put all my valuables: in my oversize lockbox at the bank," she responded while giving Benjamin the scrap of paper she had pulled from her purse.

"Damn thing should never have been sent here, if you ask me," said a voice from the kitchen.

"Now, Ethel, we talked about this," said Brandy.

"I'm just saying," Ethel said.

"No, she is absolutely right; we should never have sent it to you. If we had thought for one minute it would put you in harm's way, or if I had thought of putting it in the bank on such short notice like you did, you would never have received it. Putting it in the bank was an outstanding idea," Phillip said.

"Sorry," said Franky. "I didn't think of that either."

Ethel returned after starting the pot of coffee and putting the teakettle on. "Tea or coffee?" she asked Shawn.

"Oh, nothing, please. I am waiting for the bathroom as well."

Ethel looked over at Benjamin, who said, "Coffee, please."

Then she turned to Franky, who said, "Tea, please."

"Tea for me as well, please," Phillip said.

"Got ya," responded Ethel, returning to the kitchen. Over her shoulder, she said, "That book is a grimoire, isn't it?"

Brandy turned with a puzzled look on her face.

"Yes," responded Phillip without any hesitation.

"Is it one of the three Grand Grimoires?" asked Ethel.

"What are you two talking about? What the hell is a grimoire?" Brandy said.

Phillip ignored her question and instead answered Ethel. "Yes, it is."

"So they do exist," responded Ethel.

"How do you know about the books?" Benjamin asked, unsuccessfully trying to hide his bewilderment.

"I am from New Orleans, a city known for witches. Those books are feared by some but highly sought after by others who mean to bring evil forces to bear. I always thought them a fairy tale— that is, until I felt the power this one generated from the backseat as we rode over to the bank."

"Are you a witch?" asked Shawn with no judgment in his voice.

Ethel hesitated as she poured the now-steaming water from the kettle into cups. "No, I am not a witch, but I come from a family in which certain members took up voodoo. I tried my whole life to distance myself from them and their beliefs."

"Hello! Again, what the hell is a grimoire?" asked Brandy. They had all forgotten her question as they talked.

"A book of spells, my dear," responded Phillip.

"And the Grand Grimoires are like the king of grimoires?" Brandy said.

"Well, yes, I guess you can say that," said Phillip. Then he continued with Ethel. "I would like to know more about what you know when we get a chance."

"Well, sweetheart, there is not enough time in this world for me to tell you all of what I know," Ethel joked.

"I meant about—"

"I know what you meant. I am just pulling on one of those skinny little chicken legs of yours." With that, Ethel started to deliver the drink orders.

Franky could not keep the grin off his face.

Josette, who was making her way down the hall, stopped at Ethel and whispered, "You have the most beautiful spirit standing next to you."

"So you have the gift," Ethel responded in a whisper.

"Yes, and I think you have some gifts of your own, don't you?" Josette asked.

Ethel simply gave her a smile and continued to deliver drinks.

After a few minutes of shuffling and bathroom breaks, the group finally all gathered in the kitchen. "Now that we are all here, we need to start talking about our next steps," said Phillip, taking the lead. "I know we need to get what information we can from Benjamin's private eye before we devise a plan of attack, but for now, I am more worried about our plan for defense. We need to stay together or in small groups at all times. Joe is out there, and we don't know what he is capable of. I have no doubt he had a hand in Hoffman's murder, so don't think for a moment he would hesitate to kill one of us if he had the chance."

"And how do you suggest we stay together?" asked Brandy, not liking where the conversation was going.

"Brandy, I know what you are going to say, but you need to come with us to the hotel tonight. It is just too dangerous for you to stay here," said Phillip, bracing himself for her response.

"Only if Ethel comes too," she said.

Phillip was shocked. He had spent the whole trip trying to figure out how to tell Brandy she would need to leave her home. Her response came so quickly that he knew she too had been working the situation out in her head for some time.

"Of course she can come," Benjamin said, not waiting for Phillip to respond. "I am paying for everything, so please, you are both welcome."

Everyone turned his or her attention to Ethel, who had yet to reply. Reaching out, she took Brandy's hand. "Where she goes, I go," she said.

"Do you mind following us to the hotel? The rentals are packed. It's just a short way up to Brandon," said Phillip.

"Sure, not a problem," said Brandy.

"Well, actually, I was hoping you could take Ethel's car. At least Joe may think you are still home."

"Of course," said Ethel. "I would rather take my Cadillac than her old car anyway."

For a while, everyone just sat there, not knowing what to say. Then Mary spoke up. "If it is okay, I can present what little data I was able to collect in Dublin. It's not much, but—"

"That's fine, Mary. Anything," responded Phillip, not sure what else to say.

"Well, I did some digging on Hoffman's request; it seems the house was indeed built by a man named Banthom—Chadwick Banthom, to be exact. However, a few months earlier, the land was purchased not by a Chadwick Banthom but by one Gunari Danior. It seems he changed his name."

Everyone at the table sat quietly, turning his or her full attention to Mary.

"There was not a lot to go on, but I thought it may help somehow," Mary said, leaning back in her chair.

"Danior? What kind of name is that?" asked Benjamin.

"I looked that up too," said Mary, pulling a small notepad from her purse. She flipped through the pages until she found what she was looking for. "It's Romany."

"So he was really a Gypsy," said Phillip.

"I believe so, yes," Mary said. "The first name means 'Warrior.'"

"And the last?" Franky said.

"'Born with teeth,'" responded Mary. "Sorry, but that is all I have."

"He was making sure no one knew his heritage. A Gypsy back then may have been hard pressed to explain his status, especially one with enough money to buy land and build a fine home upon it," Franky said.

"Well done, Mary," said Phillip, obviously impressed.

"He may have been a witch before he even got to Ireland," said Ethel. "Gypsies are known for being natural witches."

"Sorry, but you've lost me," said Benjamin.

"Look," said Ethel, "there are some things about witches that are just known. There are different kinds of witches: those who naturally possess the power to manipulate spirits and those who achieve the power from other means, like making a deal with the devil."

"What do you mean manipulate spirits?" asked Josette, leaning in.

"Magic is not something witches do on their own; their power comes from their ability to manipulate the spirit world. Spirits are all around us. There are those that can't pass on because they need to tell us something or need to prove something. There are those that simply are not ready to give up life, those that don't even know they're dead, and those that have no sense of being left or the knowledge there is someplace else to go next. You can see and hear those spirits, my dear—at least the ones who want you to see them. There are always more that will never be seen."

On Josette's face was a look of confusion.

"Look, what do you use to clear a house?" Ethel asked.

"Sage, of course."

"Do you clean the whole house or just the spirit?"

"Why, the whole house," said Josette. Then came the epiphany. "Now I get you. So even someone like me will never see all the spirits around us. My gift is only for those who want to be seen."

"Yes, but someone like me can still feel them around whether they want to be seen or not, and a witch can manipulate them to do their will. A witch, with that power and the right words or the right potions, can be a tremendous force." Ethel took a long pause. "But satanic witches—that is a different story. Their power comes from a very dark and evil source. By completing certain rituals that mock the power of Holy Communion and the Trinity, they move beyond the ability to simply manipulate spirits to the power to command them. They are far more powerful." Ethel paused again. "Lastly, there is the most powerful witch of all. If certain acts are done—I don't know what all that involves, and I don't want to—a witch can command not only human spirits but also spirits that were never in human form."

"Demons!" said Mary, speaking more to herself than to anyone else in the room.

"That is what I believe our friend here is trying to achieve, and only the book, the one of which you spoke just a moment ago, could give him the right words and potions to make it happen. And that is why he needs to be stopped and, for God's sake, never get his hands on it," Ethel said.

"Why not burn it or rip it apart or something?" Shawn asked.

"Please. If you'll indulge me for a moment," said Benjamin, "I would like to convey some family secrets. My ancestor Sister Margret Mary tried to burn one of the books once, but when she put the flame to it, it was she who was burned alive, and the book remained unharmed. Then there was another relative—for the life of me, I can't remember that Burk's name. Anyway, he tried to tear through one with a pair of scissors, only it was his throat that got cut, not the book." Benjamin shook his head. "No, I don't think the books can be destroyed, but they can be contained."

At that moment, someone knocked on the front door, causing everyone at the table to jump. After taking a few seconds to catch his breath, Benjamin got up. "It must be Tony," he said, and he trotted over to the door. He let in a large

Hispanic gentleman standing a good six foot five. He looked to be in his mid to late forties and had broad shoulders and a muscular build. "Everyone, this is Tony Alvarez, the acquaintance I told you about on the flight over here. He will be doing our investigative work while we are here."

As Benjamin made introductions one by one to the group, the distraction seemed to brighten the mood. Once introductions were completed, Benjamin excused himself and walked his guest out onto the front step, where they could be seen talking in the doorway.

"He stays in our room," joked Brandy.

"I would let him check under my bed anytime," Ethel said. "That is one good-looking hunk of man there."

"Behave yourselves, ladies, or we will have to lock you in your rooms," said Franky.

"If he is in there, honey, you can lock me in and throw away that ever-loving key," said Ethel.

Shawn giggled.

After just a few moments, Benjamin returned alone. "He's already put a trace on Joe," he announced to the group. "But he thinks we should have Brandy and Ethel return to their homes during the day so that he doesn't suspect we are on to him. If he shows, Tony will tail him."

"Do you trust this guy?" asked Phillip.

"Well, to tell you the truth, Phillip, he's already

looked in your underwear drawer," said Benjamin with a smile.

"What do you mean by that?" said Phillip.

"He is the man I hired years ago to search your house on numerous occasions," Benjamin said.

"I knew it! I knew someone had been in my house!" exclaimed Phillip. He did not appear angry but seemed more relieved that he was not crazy.

"Not to change the subject, but I think a man should be with them when they come back," Shawn said, nodding toward the two elderly women. "If they arrive before light and don't leave until dark, they will need to stay inside, of course, but he won't know a man is even there."

"I agree," said Franky. "I am not ready to put their safety solely in the hands of a stranger. What if he gets a lead or something and leaves to follow it up? I'll come back with them tomorrow."

"Well, I was hoping to get further along with our plans tonight, but I know we are all exhausted," Phillip said, looking at Benjamin, who was finishing a loud yawn. "Franky will come back tomorrow with Brandy and Ethel. I know he is dying to spend time with Brandy anyway. Then we will rotate daily, if that sounds good to everyone."

"Just let me grab a few things, and we can go," said Brandy.

Mathew could see Porspoder, France, in the distance. Lights from the town dotted the outline of the coast. He had been to that small harbor more than once; he loved the small, rocky beaches that gave way to green fields and the hedgerows tucked just behind insignificant stone walls. The streets of the town were narrow, and for the most part, the houses were constructed with brown brick. It was hard to believe they had made it so far so fast; it was as if the creature below deck had threatened Poseidon himself to provide strong winds and calm seas. It was feeding time again; the master had to have his meal. Mathew knew the creature would emerge from below deck shortly, and then he would hear the sound of a splash from the side of the ship as the monster entered the water. He did not like watching him swim to shore; he had done it once while circling the southwest tip of England. There was nothing human about the way he moved through the water; it was more like watching a snake seeking dry land. When he was finished, Mathew knew he would make his way back to the ship with a body or two and then simply return below deck.

Mathew never spoke to the master unless asked to speak. He was proud to serve; since the day he'd completed the ritual himself, he'd felt stronger than he ever had. He could feel power deep inside him, a power he could not wait to exploit. It was an honor to be Banthom's servant, and Banthom had promised him the title of Judas, the second-in-command. As for Joe, Mathew did not think much of him. He was weak and unworthy of his master's trust. If given the chance, he would slit Joe's throat himself, but the master needed him.

Mathew thought he could see someone walking near the shore. *Poor bastard*, he thought to himself. If only the townspeople knew what awaited them. The master was clever. The victim's body would never be found; he would bring it back to the boat to be dumped into the ocean once they were far from shore. Last night, it had been a couple, a man and woman. They'd been young, in their mid to late twenties. Mathew had thrown them off the ship early the next morning. It was obvious each meal had a direct effect on the master. He was becoming more and more human each time. If they continued with their middle-of-the-night stops along the way, he figured his master would conform into something completely different, something magnificent, long before they reached the shores of Florida.

It was late when the troop finally arrived at the hotel, a modest three-story structure off Interstate 75 just north of Brandon. *The Fireside—what a cozy name for such a generic hotel*, thought Josette.

Benjamin had made all the arrangements: they would occupy three two-bedroom suites on the top floor, all next to each other, with doors that opened between each suite. It was nice and clean, with blue-and-green-patterned carpet and oversize paintings of different flowers hanging from the walls. The group had decided to keep the doors open at all times. In the first room, Mary and Benjamin would share with Phillip and Josette. Ethel would be with Brandy in the middle room, and Shawn and Franky would be at the end.

Sitting in bed with Phillip sound asleep on the bed next to her, Josette waited patiently for her spirit guide to appear. It had not shown itself for the past three nights, the nights she had spent with Phillip, and she worried it would not show this time. Maybe it would only appear if she was alone. It was hard to say with spirits.

In the morning, they would all meet to plan their course of action. Josette wanted to help give them direction. She needed whatever information the spirit might offer. Still, she was so exhausted from the long trip she could barely keep her eyes open.

The room suddenly felt different. It was swaying back and forth, and out of nowhere, Josette could acutely smell the ocean air. The room gradually faded into a foggy mist, and she could hear the sound of waves slapping against the bow of a ship. Had her guide come at last? If so, this was something completely new.

Looking around, she noticed she was no longer lying down but standing. The floor was gently moving back and forth, only now it was not a floor but the deck of a sailboat. Standing in the night air, she saw the figure of a man less than five feet away. He stood tall and had long, flowing brown hair. She seemed to go unnoticed, for the man did not turn or make any indication to acknowledge her presence. She looked around; there was nothing but open ocean as far as she could see, but she seemed to know just where she was: she was off the coast of France. How she knew that, she was not sure. Maybe her connection with Banthom was stronger than she'd thought, or maybe her guide was showing her glimpses of what was going on. She was not sure.

"I will make you a deal." A sour voice came from the man standing in front of her. "Get out of my head, and I will let you live."

Josette looked around, and since there was not another soul anywhere, she assumed he was talking to her. Slowly, she moved back, not bothering to turn.

"I will not make this deal again," he said. "One last time, get out of my fucking head, you bitch." With that, the man turned and lunged, only now it wasn't a man at all. Even in the darkness, she could see its large, pointed white teeth bearing down on her. She screamed into the open air.

"Josette! Josette, wake up," Phillip said, sounding worried. "Are you okay? It's just a dream."

Josette buried her face into his chest and sobbed. "My God, Phillip, I don't know that we can do this."

CHAPTER 12

A WARNING

Franky sat back on the couch in his room and sighed. It would not be long before the nightmare began. He had taken notice from the start of the adventure that the group had broken into pairs—Phillip with Josette, Benjamin with Mary, Brandy with Ethel, and he with Shawn—and not much had changed over the past six weeks, though the group's bonds had gotten stronger, even more so between the pairs. He was happy for Phillip; Josette seemed to be his ideal partner. He had never seen him so happy, and now that he was moving on to a new career, he had the comfort of knowing Phillip was moving on as well.

As for Mary and Benjamin, they seemed to be having the time of their lives, even with all the doom and gloom hovering over everyone. Those who were not on old-lady watch back at the trailer had a lot of free time on their hands, and they were all getting overly tan from too much time at the pool.

Just that morning at the pool, Josette had had a long talk with Shawn about Samantha, his girlfriend who'd passed away. She'd told him that she had seen her and that Samantha never left his side. Josette had said Samantha was worried about him and would not leave until she knew he was okay.

"You need to move on, Shawn, so she can move on," Josette had told him.

Franky had felt his pain as Shawn broke down and cried while nodding in acknowledgment, seeming to understand just what she meant.

"As long as she feels you need her, she will stay, but once you take a step to move on with your life, she will move on as well," Josette had said, holding him close to her.

That was a life-changing moment for Shawn, thought Franky. Already Shawn seemed different, more willing to allow some happiness into his life. Franky was pleased to have been there to see the transformation. Shawn was slowly becoming Franky's best buddy. They enjoyed hanging out together, and even though they had shared the same room for six weeks, they never once had gotten angry or argued. Thinking back, Franky realized that other than Phillip, he'd never truly had any friends, and he couldn't remember any

even close to his own age. Shawn had shown him
what it was like to be young.

Though Franky had to admit the group had a
lot of free time on their hands, every night, they
came back to reality when the nightly meetings
were held. That was when they talked about
Banthom, what they needed to defeat him, and
what they needed to do to survive.

They had traded in the rental cars for a Ford
panel van and a Chevy pickup. The van hid many
of the tools they would take into battle, including
twenty-two gas cans filled with petrol. They'd
supplied themselves with crosses, salt, sage,
holy water, Bibles, and everything else in Father
McDonald's manual they could get their hands on,
even though they were not sure how they were to
use all of the items. Hemlock, it seemed, was not
easy to get, so they had to do without it.

It had taken a full two weeks for Tony to find
Joe's location. He was staying at a small dive of a
motel on Old US 41, just south of Gibsonton. The
way Tony described it, Franky thought it was one
of those places in Florida that would have been
an ideal location for northern tourists thirty years
ago. Franky had seen many such locations while
driving the old highways. They were in need of
drastic repair, and those living on the fringe of
society rented most of the rooms. Such a place
was a home for many and an hourly rental for

others. Once on Joe's tail, Tony said he had never once let him out of his sight. Tony would call in his report to the group nightly with details of Joe's daily movements. It seemed that during the day, Joe stayed in a location by the clubhouse in Mrs. Cartwright's community, where he would spy on her house with a pair of binoculars. Once, when Brandy and Ethel where leaving for church, he had driven right up in Brandy's drive and then seemed to chicken out. After that, the male escorts had stayed at Ethel's instead, in case he ever got the nerve to go inside. Other days, he was in Ruskin, where Tony discovered his aunt and uncle owned a restaurant. However, it was Tony's talk about the time Joe spent roaming the same back road near the town of Riverview that got Franky's attention. If Banthom was to make shore, he would need a place to hide, thought Franky—a place to carry out his quest for the book.

Only after Tony gave them the all clear each night would the group in the trailers return for the night. Then came time for the nightly meeting, during which they worked on their strategy for dealing with the imminent conflict with Banthom. They closely worked out every scenario. What if he brought a newly created coven assembled on his travels? How could they protect Brandy and still not be seen? Throughout all their discussions, one thing was certain: Joe was the key. Eventually, he would point them to his master. If they could find where Banthom planned to hide, they would bar the doors; set it aflame; and burn the location, Banthom, the assassin, and, if need be, Joe all at once. Except they didn't even know where Joe was. Tony had called Benjamin that morning and said Joe left in the middle of the night. Tony was at Mrs. Cartwright's, waiting and hoping he would show.

At the end of the night came Josette's update. Every night since she'd gotten to the hotel, she'd dreamed, suffering through nightmares, each one worse than the night before. She was worn out—everyone could see it—but every night, she got more information about the creature's location. While everyone wanted her nightmares to end, none could wait to find out how long they had left before the creature descended upon them. According to Josette's report last night, it would not be long. Banthom and his friend were just off the coast of Naples, and still, the group was no closer to knowing his plans than they had been on day one. After talking with Josette that morning, Franky knew the group would be even more despondent when they realized she had nothing new to add. Last night had been dreamless, with no connection made. Like Joe's, Banthom's location was a mystery.

Franky looked at the clock and then yelled to Shawn, who was taking a nap in his room, "It's eight thirty! We need to get going. Phillip called, and he is already on his way back from Brandy's."

Joe had figured out someone was tailing him a good week before he acted. Day after day, he went to the old lady's trailer and watched, knowing that he too was being watched. He had to be careful and act as if he did not know about the large Hispanic gentleman in the gray car. He stopped his trips to Riverview, however; maybe the man had not been following him that long. Last night, after receiving the call from Mathew in Naples, he'd made his move. At two in the morning, he'd gotten up, sneaked out to his car, and pulled away. For the next ten miles, his eyes had been glued to the rearview mirror. He had not seen a single set of lights behind him. He had given his pursuer the slip. Finally, confident enough he was not being followed, he'd slipped onto Interstate 75 and dashed down to Naples to pick up his cargo.

Just before sunrise, they'd been back with Banthom nicely stowed away. Joe had marveled at how much he had already changed. His face looked almost normal; his speech was much improved; and most of all, he seemed more human, as if with one more good meal, he would be complete. Driving now, Joe felt exhausted, but there was a lot of work to be done, and there was no time for sleep. If everything went just right, by tomorrow they would have Banthom's book, and he would have Mary. Still, Joe frowned as he drove with Mathew. How clever he had been, and how well he had planned; however, with the failure to find what he needed at that old bitch's trailer, he was afraid it might all fall through. Still, there was the hotel. The master had pointed them right to where the old women were staying and where they needed to go next.

"The wench got in my head, but I got in her head as well," Banthom had said when asked how he knew where the group from Dublin was gathered. Joe had no idea what he was talking about, but he knew better than to question.

For that night's meeting, Benjamin had gone out of his way to secure a private section of the restaurant downstairs that was usually reserved for private parties. That way, they could all enjoy a late dinner while conducting business. The room was large, with a formal dining room table in the center and large, scenic windows on two sides. The all-white walls were highlighted with deep blue curtains and gold-leaf wall art depicting various kinds of sea life. It was nine thirty when Brandy and Ethel arrived; they were always the last to arrive to meetings because they needed to settle in for a minute after returning to the hotel. They'd all agreed the night before that today was their last day of returning to the trailer; it was getting too close to the time when Banthom was due to arrive, and the group needed to stay together until they were ready to strike. Before they could all even take their seats, the hotel staff were carrying in plates of shrimp, T-bones, and mixed vegetables. To accompany the food, five bottles of champagne sat on the table, chilling in buckets of ice. Everyone seemed in good spirits. Somehow, they all seemed to know that time was short, and they might not get the chance to enjoy themselves again as a group for some time.

After dinner, Tony came in for his nightly update. He usually gave his reports by phone, but with Joe gone and Banthom so close, Benjamin had asked him to give his update personally. As he walked into the room, he smiled his greeting to the group. The look on his face was discerning, to say the least.

"Please have a seat, Tony. Would you like a plate?" Benjamin said.

"No, no, I am fine," he replied, taking a seat next to Benjamin. "I am sorry, but I have not been able to locate Mr. Chung. I spent the day at Mrs. Cartwright's house, but he never showed. After that, I went by his uncle's restaurant and then back to the motel to see if he'd returned." He turned to

Brandy and talked to her directly. "Before I came here, I made one more pass past your house, Mrs. Cartwright. When I got there, I noticed the front door was ajar, so I went in. The back window was broken, and the place had been ransacked. I am so sorry. If I had just stayed awhile after you left, I would have caught him in the act."

"No, don't you even worry yourself about that," said Brandy. "That bastard would have gotten in one way or the other. Just thank God he waited till we all left. I don't want anyone getting hurt."

"Well, thank you," replied Tony. "I just feel like I have let everyone down. I have little doubt he made me. He was not waiting for just you to leave but me as well."

"You told me the very first night that tailing someone for that long would be hard and almost impossible without being seen," said Benjamin, reassuring Tony. "You've done outstanding work, and no one at this table is going to think you let anyone down."

With that, everyone at the table gave Tony statements of reassurance.

"Well, thank you. You are a great group of people," said Tony with a broad smile. "Even if I have no idea what the hell you are all up to, I am sure it is for something good. I plan to go to his uncle's restaurant tomorrow; maybe I can dig up something there."

"I would like to go with you if that is okay," said Franky. "We don't have to go to the trailer anymore, and I feel like I have to do something."

Tony looked over at Franky and seemed to ponder the suggestion in his head. "You know, that may be helpful, if the group has no objections," he said, looking across the table. Seeing no dissenters, he continued. "I'll pick you up around lunchtime then—say, eleven thirty?"

"Sounds good to me," replied Franky.

Brandy said, "Phillip, I've got to go home and—"

"No, Brandy, I know what you are going to say," Phillip said. "I know you feel you need to, but we will all go over in the morning together."

"But—"

"But nothing," Franky said, supporting Phillip's stand. "It's just not safe."

"I locked everything up when I left," Tony said. "You can call the police in the morning and tell them you just came home and found it that way."

"Fine," Brandy huffed.

"What about my place? Did you check that?" asked Ethel, wringing her hands while waiting for an answer.

"There were no signs of a break-in there. The doors were still locked, and no windows were broken. I think you are all right," replied Tony. "Now, I really must be going. I am going to run past the motel one more time tonight just to make sure he does not come back."

"Tony," said Benjamin as the investigator got up to leave, "remember, under no circumstances are you to make direct contact with this man or anyone he may be with. I know you don't know everything that is going on here, but trust me on this one."

Tony looked at Benjamin and saw a look of concern. "I promise. No contact, just surveillance like we agreed." With that, he nodded his goodbyes to the group and left.

"He's a good man. You did a great job in finding us help," said Phillip, patting Benjamin on the shoulder. "Let's just hope he picks up Joe's tail again."

No one had noticed Shawn climbing onto the chair and onto the table. It was not until he was standing in the middle of the table that all heads turned toward him. Without a word, he undid his belt buckle, unbuttoned his jeans, unzipped the fly, pulled down his pants and then his underwear, took his penis in his right hand, and started urinating directly on Benjamin's lap.

"You like this, don't you, you spoiled, rich little prick?" he shouted as Benjamin leaped out of the line of fire. "And this is for your whore," Shawn added as he turned his aim at Mary, but Mary had already risen and moved well out of his range. Still, he continued speaking to her. "Your little Chinese friend wants to sodomize you. Did you know that?" Then, with a hideous chuckle, he added, "But with that little cock of his, I doubt a girl like you would even notice."

"Shawn!" exclaimed Phillip. "What the hell are you doing?"

Shawn finished pissing on Mary's empty seat, shook his shaft, and then turned and faced him. "Phillip Parker. You cocksucker, you will pay for killing the Judas. I have special plans for you."

"My God, look at his eyes," said Franky. Everyone turned to look at his eyes: they were beet red, and from them tears of blood formed and then slipped down his face.

"And you, Mr. Lake," said Shawn, turning to him. "Maybe I will save you for last so you can watch the rest die before you, just like that cunt mother of yours."

"Banthom is here. He is standing outside this building as we speak," said Josette. "I feel him just outside the room."

"Bitch, I warned you to stay out of my head!" yelled Shawn, this time in a completely different voice, deeper and rougher. He grabbed one of the empty champagne bottles and, without a moment's hesitation, sent it flying through the air. It hit the still-seated Josette squarely on the forehead, shattering with the impact. Josette at once went limp and fell to the floor, hitting with a loud thump.

Laughter, dark and demented, filled the room. Shawn started to float just above the table with his arms outstretched as if some invisible force were trying to tear him in half.

While the others stared in amazement, Mary acted. She reached into her bag and produced the small vial of holy water they were all now required to carry. She pulled off the top and threw it, bottle and all, at the hovering Shawn. He let out a loud scream of pain as the water seemed to slice his skin open where it landed. The other women took the hint, reached into their purses, and produced their bottles of holy water as well.

"I will kill you all!" Shawn screamed, and before any of them could pull the caps off the holy-water bottles, he came crashing down onto the table, where he lay motionless.

Phillip and Mary dashed over to Josette. Ethel and Brandy were already by her side on the floor.

"She's breathing, but she is out cold," said Brandy.

"She's got a strong pulse," said Ethel.

Phillip just stood there in shock, not saying a word.

"Her head's bleeding pretty badly. Look at that glass stuck in her scalp," said Mary. "She needs to go to the hospital."

Just then, the last two remaining restaurant staff, a man dressed like a cook and a woman dressed like a waitress, ran into the room.

"What the hell is going on in here?" asked the man.

"Call for help! We need an ambulance!" Brandy yelled at him.

"Look, I don't know what's going on, but—"

"We need an ambulance now!" Ethel screamed at him. With that, he turned and ran off.

"Do you have any clean cloths we can cover her head with?" Mary asked the woman.

"We have some clean tablecloths," she replied.

"That will be fine," said Brandy.

While everyone else was checking on Josette, Franky was the only one to go to Shawn. He was dazed and semilethargic. After checking his eyes, Franky pulled up his underwear and pants, buttoned them for him, and then pulled Shawn into a sitting position. "You okay?" he asked, but he got no response. Franky knew what it was like to be a living puppet for those foul creatures. Fritz had used the same method on him years ago in Michigan. To that day, he would wake up some nights screaming after dreaming of losing control of himself to something evil, something so powerful it could push him to the side and use his body as it wished. In that position, one could see everything but do nothing. Slowly, he helped

Shawn down off the table. Franky could see a good-sized goose egg forming on his head. "How is you head? Do you need to lie down?" Franky asked.

"No, I just want to go to my room. I'm feeling a little sick to my stomach," Shawn replied. "How is Josette?" he asked as he started to walk over to the others with Franky holding on to him.

"You're kinda unstable. You sure you don't need to sit?" Franky asked, afraid Shawn would fall without support.

"No, I'm fine," he replied.

"Oh my God, Shawn, I forgot about you," said Phillip, looking up at last. "Does he need to go to the hospital as well?"

"No, I think he will be fine," said Franky.

By the time Shawn and Franky made it to the other side of the table, the others had worked out a plan. Phillip would ride to the hospital with Josette in the ambulance. Mary would take Ethel's car and follow so they would have a car there when they needed to leave. The others would go back to their rooms, where they would stay behind the salt lines until dawn.

Joe's heart was pounding in his chest. For the first time since he had started that adventure, he started to question his sanity. In the past few minutes, he'd watched two cold-blooded murders take place. As they'd made the turn into their parking space, Joe had spotted the man who was tailing him coming out of the hotel and heading for his car. He'd pointed him out to Mathew, and without a moment's hesitation, Mathew had walked over to the man, who was bending over to unlock his car door. Before the man had even turned the key, Mathew had slit his throat wide open. He had been so quick Joe was sure no one had seen a thing. Mathew had finished unlocking the door, thrown the man inside, and then nonchalantly closed the door. Joe was amazed at how easy he had made it look.

The pair had wasted no time in walking through the hotel lobby and into the elevator, which they'd taken up to the third floor. As soon the doors had opened, Joe had noticed that something caught Mathew's eye, and instead of turning left toward the room number Banthom had given them, Mathew had taken a right, following a pretty young housekeeper who had just stopped her cart and was letting herself into an empty room. Without a sound, Mathew had gone up behind the girl, snapped her neck, dragged her inside the empty room, and come out as if everything were completely normal. He'd closed the door. In his hand had dangled the young woman's badge.

"Just in case they are not home," Mathew had said with a devious grin.

Joe thought he might be able to find a way to relieve his guilt from watching Hoffman and the private eye die, but that girl had known nothing about what was going on. She'd just been in the wrong place at the wrong time. How quickly her life had been taken from her. Joe started to feel sick. All he could do was carry on, though, because if he showed any hesitation, he could be gone just as quickly. He wondered how they would deal with the group if they were still in their rooms. Would Mathew slaughter them all at once? *What if they have guns?* he wondered.

Joe felt a large sense of relief when they opened the door to where Josette, Phillip, Mary, and Benjamin were staying and found no one there. Joe gently pushed the thin salt line away with his foot, not for himself but for Mathew who was no longer fully human. Joe wondered what the cleaning staff must have thought when seeing that on the floor each morning.

Joe was gushing with relief. Once they were inside, it only took a matter of minutes to find what they were looking for. Joe had a good idea where to look the moment he walked in. They spent the rest of the time trashing the place, making sure they hit all three rooms equally. If the group got an idea of what they were really after, the plan might not work. Once they had completed the level of dumping, spilling, and scattering they desired, they left the room and headed back to the elevator. Joe looked at the door where he knew the body of the young girl lay, and a chill went down his spine.

As they headed for the lobby and the front door of the hotel, they stopped and headed the other way. Outside was an ambulance with its flashing lights cutting into the night air. The last thing they needed was a delay; they had more work to do, this time on a lonesome road in Riverview.

Benjamin was the first to enter the rooms. "They have been here, I see," he said in disappointment. "That fucking Joe must have broken the salt line."

Ethel and Brandy came in next, followed by Franky, who was still propping up Shawn.

"Well, what a great night this turned out to be," Benjamin said, walking over to the couch in his suite. With one hand, he cleared a spot. "Have Shawn lie here, where we can keep an eye on him."

Ethel and Brandy did not say a word but walked directly to their own suite. "They hit in here as well," Brandy said from the next room.

Franky laid Shawn on the couch and then made his way toward his and Shawn's suite. "Same thing here," he said.

"Well, at least we know he didn't get the book

here," replied Ethel, walking back into Benjamin's suite with Brandy. "And from what I can see, they didn't do any damage, just made one hell of a mess."

Benjamin had told the hotel staff that he did not need or want any room service. The salt on the floors was their protection. He didn't want them coming in and sweeping it all away, and there was no way to explain their reasoning for the salt to them. The Joe factor was becoming more than he could bear. Obviously, he had not completed the ritual yet, so he was still completely human and unaffected by anything they might use against Banthom and his friend. "If it wasn't for that damn Joe, they would have never gotten in."

"There is no sense in worrying about it now, dear," said Brandy, bending over to pick up some clothes thrown across the floor. "May as well get started picking up this mess."

"It can wait till morning," said Benjamin. However, Brandy paid no heed to him and continued what she was doing.

"If you think for one minute she is going to go to bed with a mess like this that needs taken care of, you're crazy," said Ethel. "Might as well get your head down and buns up and start digging, baby." With that, Shawn made a feeble attempt to get off the couch. "Not you, sweetie. Sorry, but the way you look, we will be picking you up, and I'm too old for that," said Ethel.

"We'll start in this room and make our way to Franky and Shawn's," said Brandy.

Josette woke up just before midnight to find Phillip sitting next to her, holding his hand in hers. "Phillip," she said softly.

"Josette, oh, thank God you're awake," he responded with tears in his eyes.

"How long have I been here?" she asked, looking around the room.

"A couple hours at least," answered Phillip. "We were so worried about you."

"How did I get here?" she asked. "Did you bring me?"

"You came by ambulance. I just got in to see you a little while ago. They said they were running tests. I think they did a CT scan."

"That bloody bastard nailed me good," she said, trying to sit up.

"Please lie back down. You took one hell of a hit. The nurse said it took them forever to get all the glass out of your head."

"Will you ask the nurse for some water? I need something," Josette said, ignoring Phillip's request and pulling herself to a sitting position.

Phillip stood to get the nurse, but at that exact moment, a nurse walked in and smiled.

"So you decided to wake up. I need to get your vitals, dear."

"Did all her tests come back okay?" asked Phillip, moving out of the way of the nurse. "Is she going to be all right?"

"I'm sure she will be fine. The doctor will be in around seven. That's when he usually makes his rounds," she responded, giving them another smile.

Mary, who was fast asleep in the chair across the room, awoke.

"Mary! She's awake!" said Phillip joyfully.

Mary jumped up and walked over to Josette's bed. "We have been so worried about you, girl."

"Mary, how nice of you to come," said Josette, slightly slurring her words.

"I'm sorry, but I am going to ask both of you to leave for just a little while. The cafeteria is on the third floor, if you need some fresh coffee," said the nurse. "It will only take me a few minutes."

"Coffee sounds wonderful," said Mary. "Come on, Phillip. Walk with me. You need a break." Reluctantly, he agreed.

CHAPTER 13

BY THE MORNING LIGHT

The sun was just starting to peek through the white blinds in Josette's room when Phillip caught himself from falling over in his chair. He had unintentionally fallen asleep.

"Go back to the hotel," said Josette, who was wide awake and watching the morning news on the TV hanging from the wall at the foot of her bed. "You and Mary both need your rest."

"I want to hear what the doctor says," said Phillip, stretching his arms in the air.

"Look, I have a phone right over there," she replied, pointing to the phone sitting on her nightstand. "I promise to call you the minute I hear anything."

"But what if he comes for you again?" said Phillip with worry on his face.

"Look, I am perfectly safe here. There are plenty of people around. I don't think even he would be that bold. Now, go."

"Where is Mary anyway?" he asked.

Just then, he heard a loud flush coming from the bathroom. After a few seconds, Mary came out, looking ruffled. "Oh, you're awake," she said to Phillip. "Did you know you snore like a bear?"

"Mary, talk some sense into this man. You two need to go back to the hotel. God only knows what's happened since you've been gone. They all need you more than I do right now. I am feeling much better. Please convince him to go," Josette said.

"Okay, okay, I can take a hint. You just want to get rid of me," joked Phillip.

"Finally, you get it," said Josette, raising her arms in the air. "I thought I would have to throw a bottle your way to get it through that thick skull."

"All right, all right," said Phillip. "You ready to go, Mary?"

"More than ready," said Mary, who walked over and kissed Josette on the cheek. "You are one strong lady."

"Thank you, and thank you for being here," she replied.

Phillip got out of his chair and then bent down and gave her a kiss. "Remember to call me as soon as the doctor leaves."

Josette made a crossing motion across her chest. "I cross my heart."

As Phillip and Mary walked through the hospital, Phillip thought about how natural everything seemed. *These people have no idea of the darkness that is out there*, he thought. Lucky for them, they could go along with their busy lives, not worrying about such evil things. How he wished he could have that same feeling again.

Outside, the morning sun was already beating down. It was going to be a hot one for sure. Though reluctant to leave, Phillip knew he needed a nice shower and a long nap. Hopefully the group back at the hotel was okay. He had been so worried about Josette he had forgotten to call them to fill them in on Josette's condition, as he'd promised. As they walked, Mary looked over her shoulder. Phillip caught her more than once.

"What's wrong?" asked Phillip. "You seem a little spooked."

"Nothing," said Mary. "It's just, well, you know how you sometimes feel like you're being watched or something?"

Just then, a large man walked toward them from the opposite direction, pulled a gun out, and pointed it directly at Phillip's face. "You were the last thing on my master's list," he said. "How lucky to find you both in once place."

"What do you want?" asked Phillip.

"Just unlock your car," the man said.

Then came the sound of someone else coming up from behind. It was Joe. "Do what he says, Phillip. I don't want either one of you to get hurt." He too had a gun in his hand.

"Fuck you, Joe," said Mary.

"That's what I was promised," Joe snapped. "Now, get in the goddamn car. Mary, you're up front with me. Phillip, get in back with my friend here."

"How did you even know we were here?" asked Mary as she reluctantly got into the car.

"A little birdy told me," Joe replied with a big smile on his face.

Franky awoke to the sound of the phone on his nightstand. It took a moment for him to recognize the sound before he reached over to retrieve the phone from the cradle.

"Hello?" he said, still half asleep.

"Franky, it's Josette," said the voice on the other end.

"Josette," said Franky, pulling himself to the side of the bed. "How are you feeling? That was one hell of a hit you took."

"Much better. Is Phillip there yet?" she asked.

"Don't really know. I just woke up. Let me check in your suite; he might be in there. Hold on." After putting the phone down, he put on some shorts and walked through Brandy and Ethel's suite. No one was awake there. Then he went into the one occupied by Benjamin. No one was stirring anywhere. "Nope, everyone here is still sleeping," he replied once he got back to his own room.

"Well, I didn't think they could have made it back yet, but I thought I would try. Have him call me, will you? The doctor came in just after he left."

"What did he say?" Franky asked. Phillip was supposed to have called last night, but he never had.

"He says I have one hell of a concussion, but there is no brain swelling. I have to stay here another day for observation. I got fifteen stitches to the head."

"Wow! So how are you feeling? Are you in a lot of pain?"

"Some, but it could be worse."

"Are they giving you something for it?"

"Well, let's just say they are doing all they can." Josette spoke with a slight hesitation. "Please have Phillip call as soon as he gets in, will you?"

"Absolutely," Franky said. "The moment he walks in."

"Thanks. It's so nice to hear your voice. Talk to you soon," Josette said.

"You too," said Franky, and then he hung up the phone. In the other room, he heard someone stirring, so he pulled on a shirt and walked over to find Ethel starting a pot of coffee.

"Was that you I heard out here a minute ago?" she asked.

"Yes, Josette called and wanted to talk to Phillip, but he is not back yet," he answered.

"How did she sound?"

"Good, really. She said she had a bad concussion and needed to stay another day for observation. But she really sounded good," he answered.

"That's good," said Ethel. Then she walked over to the TV and said, "Time to turn on the news." She switched it on and then sat on the couch and waited for the coffeepot to fill.

Just then, Shawn walked in and took a seat next to Ethel. "Morning."

"Good morning, dear, and how are you feeling this morning?" Ethel asked.

"Sore. My back hurts, but I'll be okay," he said with a slight flinch.

"The way you hit that table, it's a wonder you can even walk," said Franky, taking a seat in a chair at the small, round table that made up the dining area.

As the TV came into focus, Ethel at once reached to turn up the sound. "Brandy! Brandy, you awake?"

"What's going on?" asked Franky.

"Sh," Ethel said, putting her finger to her lips.

"Now back to you, Kim," said the newscaster, and the picture changed to a lovely young lady standing in front of a weather map.

"Brandy!" yelled Ethel once again.

Benjamin walked into the room in his robe and slippers. "What's going on?" he asked Franky, who simply shrugged to show his own bewilderment.

A few seconds later, Brandy emerged from her room as well. "What do you want, Ethel?" she asked impolitely.

"What's the name of the bank you use, the one where you put the book?" Ethel asked with a large amount of enthusiasm.

"Sun City Bank. Why?"

"They just showed a picture of it on the news with all those yellow tape things around it, like the police use for a crime scene. You know what I mean," Ethel said, stumbling over her words.

"Well, what did they say?" asked Brandy.

"I don't know. They switched back to the damn weather," Ethel replied while trying to find another station with news. After three channels, she stopped. On the TV was a picture of the bank, just as Ethel had described it.

"We just found out the victim's name was Mike Banister, and he was the manager of the bank. Coworkers found him early this morning, apparently murdered by a stab wound to the back of the neck. Mr. Banister, a resident of Riverview,

Florida, had only been on the job for three months, officials say. The motive for the murder is unclear. Officials have stated the vault was not opened during the night. More on this breaking story as it continues to develop."

"Shit, Brandy, where are your keys?" asked Benjamin.

"Why, in my purse, where they always are," she responded.

"Can you check for me, please?" he asked calmly.

Brandy did not ask any questions; she got up and walked into the other room. "I must have left them at home," she said through the wall a moment later.

"He has the book," said Benjamin.

"Of course," said Franky with a look of revelation. "He did not search the trailer or the hotel rooms looking for the book; he was after the lockbox key. It takes the customer's key and the one at the bank to unlock the box. Somehow, he knew the book was at the bank. Joe must have been following the day they dropped it off."

"And remember Tony talking about his trips to Riverview? He was staking out that man's house, just waiting to get Brandy's key," said Benjamin.

"Now he has everything he needs," said Shawn. "There's no stopping him."

Josette hung up the phone after her conversation with Franky. Her head was screaming. She lay back in her bed, dealing with a thousand emotions that piled upon her like a college football gang tackle. Hearing the door to her hospital room close, she looked to see who had come in, but no one was there. She had half expected to see Phillip standing at the door, but instead, there was a small ball of light hovering just above the floor. As she watched, the ball grew, and as it grew, the light became more and more intense. When the ball reached the size of a person, it stopped. Josette knew at once her guide was back. Slowly, the light faded in the center until the only light left was a bright halo surrounding the figure of a man. For the first time, Josette could see her guide's kind face looking directly at her.

"Where have you been?" she asked with a huge sense of relief at seeing him there.

"I have been fighting the power of Gunari Danior for some time now. He has been keeping me from you. But I am nothing if not persistent."

"You mean the witch Banthom?" Josette asked.

"You must never call him by that name; you must use his Christian name. Evil uses deception for its own purpose. Only the truth will hold sway against him."

"Who are you?" asked Josette. She tried to pull

herself up to get a better look, but the pain was too great this time.

"My name is Kip Gillmore. I am a good friend of Phillip's and love him dearly," said the spirit, walking closer so Josette had no need to strain herself.

"I know who you are. Phillip talks about you all the time. He thought the world of you. Franky too."

"You must listen to me quickly, for I doubt I can fight off his force for long. He has surrounded himself with a host of evil spirits; they are everywhere," said Kip.

"What is going to happen to all of us? Will we be able to defeat this Gunari Danior?"

"The creature, like all things evil, feverously guards its true intentions, hiding behind a sea of lies. It is impossible to discern what is and is no longer truth. While he was easy to read in the beginning, now it is almost impossible. I only know that in the house in Dublin lies part of the answer: their family quest, written on a parchment hidden in the walls. I know it does no good now, but when this is all over, I feel you must find it. Gunari was the bastard son of a powerful Gypsy witch. It is said she died trying to complete this quest, and I feel Gunari is trying to take her place. Now that he has the book and needs only one more feeding to make him whole, there may be no way to stop him. I just don't know."

"He has the book?" Josette gasped. "My God, I have to tell the others."

"They already know. What they don't know is that he also has Phillip and Mary."

Josette sat straight up. Pain or no pain, she had to move. "Are they dead?' she asked, holding back tears. "For God's sake, tell me. Are they dead?"

"No, they are not dead, but I feel they will be shortly if they do not get help," said Kip, hanging his head. "You must call your friends and tell them to leave that hotel now, or I am afraid it will be some time before they can do so. The police will find Tony's body in his car very soon, along with an innocent woman lying dead in a room just down the hall." He walked over to Josette, put his hand on her midsection, and smiled. "There is always hope. There are some things you must relay to Franky if they are to have any chance." He bent over and whispered in her ear.

Brandy and Ethel emerged from their suite with suitcases in tow, which surprised the three men sitting at the table in Benjamin's suite and drinking coffee.

"What are you ladies up to?" asked Benjamin, getting up to get another cup.

"When Phillip gets here with Ethel's car, we are going home," said Brandy in a tone not to be questioned. "Benjamin, we cannot thank you enough for all you have done for us. We have spent most of this summer living like kings, and I know you sprang for everything. But it's time for me and Ethel to go home. Last night proved they can reach us no matter where we are, and we both agreed we would rather face them on our own terms in our own homes."

"Look at what happened in the restaurant last night, Benjamin," added Ethel. "We were lucky they didn't call the police."

Franky sat looking at the two women. "They have a point," he said. The phone in Franky and Shawn's room began to ring, and he ran to answer it.

"I agree," said Shawn. "Besides, I don't think we should put anyone other than ourselves in danger. We agreed to this, but the people here at the hotel don't even know what the hell is going on."

Benjamin returned with his full cup and sat down at the table. "I know. I've thought the same thing. Once Phillip returns, I think we should all leave."

"I have a two-bedroom house. Ethel has two bedrooms as well. You are all welcome to stay with us until this thing is over. He has the book now, so I don't think it will matter where we are," said Brandy, walking over to pour herself a cup of coffee. "We can prepare the same as here. Lay down your salt lines, and do whatever else we think needs done."

Just then, Franky came running back into the room. "Josette says we need to get out of here right now! She said Tony is dead and lying in the front seat of his car in the parking lot. If they find him there, we are all going to be in trouble. The staff saw him come into our little dinner party last night. We need to pack up and get the fuck out of here as fast as we can."

With that, Benjamin and Shawn both leaped up, dashed to their rooms, and started packing.

"What about Phillip and Mary?" Brandy said.

"Josette said not to worry about them. We need to pack their shit and have everyone meet at the hospital. She said she's got a lot to tell us," replied Franky, hurrying back to his own room.

Within twenty minutes, they were all downstairs in the lobby. Benjamin told Shawn and Franky to get the truck loaded while he checked out. Ethel and Brandy agreed to ride with Franky in the truck, and Shawn and Benjamin said they would follow in the van. No sooner had they loaded the back of the pickup than Benjamin came out. "We ready?" he asked.

"Packed and ready to go," said Shawn.

Pulling out of the parking lot, Franky spotted Tony's car parked in the last row farthest from the hotel. There were no other cars near his yet, but

Franky had seen posters for a job fair that started at ten that morning in one of the conference rooms, and the parking lot was already starting to fill. He pointed the car out to Ethel and Brandy. "That's Tony's car right there," he said.

"Hard to believe he is lying in there dead," said Brandy.

"He was such a nice man too," said Ethel.

CHAPTER 14

DUEL OF DEATH

Josette was just getting ready to call the nurse, when Franky popped his head around the corner. "Are you ready for visitors?" he asked.

"Oh, Franky," she replied, and she burst into tears.

Franky walked over and gave her a hug. "It's okay. We are all here."

Into the room walked Ethel and Brandy with a large vase of flowers they had purchased in the gift shop. "Oh dear, we were both so worried about you!" said Ethel, walking over and taking Josette's hand in hers.

Brandy walked to the other side of the bed and took Josette's other hand. "We need to get you home so I can take care of you."

Last came Benjamin and Shawn, who waited patiently for their chance to say their hellos, Benjamin with a kiss to the cheek and Shawn with a hug. With everyone standing around her bed, Josette broke down once more. "Sorry. It's going to take me a minute," she managed to say through her sobs.

"You take all the time you need," said Franky with his hand on her shoulder.

Finally, after a few minutes, Josette began to settle down. Waiting for them to arrive had been unbearable.

"They have Phillip and Mary," she finally blurted out before she burst back into tears.

"Oh my God," said Franky. Tears were now welling up in his eyes as well.

"They are both alive, but we need to help them," sobbed Josette.

"Okay," said Benjamin. "If Phillip were here, he would be breaking this down for us. He would make us think this through. Josette, please try to relax, and start from the beginning."

Josette took a couple deep breaths. "My spirit guide came to me a short time ago for the first time since we left Ireland." Looking up at Franky, she added, "It's Kip, Franky. He is my guide."

Franky could no longer hold back his emotions. He turned his head and started to cry. Shawn put his arm around him to reassure him.

"He said they have Phillip and Mary, but they are both alive. Where they are he did not know.

He said it was hard to get past the darkness," said Josette, trying to pull herself up.

"Let me help you, dear," said Brandy.

"He said we had to stop calling him Banthom. We need to always call him by his Christian name, Gunari Danior. Calling him anything else adds to his power of deceit. He told me he was the bastard son of a Gypsy witch, and he gave me a couple messages for Franky, though I don't know what they mean."

Franky turned back around. "What did he say?"

"Continue with the plan, and the water is by the road."

"Continue with the plan?" Franky replied. "I don't know what that means."

"I do," said Shawn. "You had planned to go with Tony today, remember?"

"The restaurant in Ruskin. That's right," said Benjamin. "You two were going to talk to Joe's aunt and uncle."

"Shit," said Franky, regaining most of his composure. "I forgot all about that with everything that happened."

"And the water by the road?" Benjamin said. "What the hell does that mean?"

They all looked at each other, waiting for someone to give an opinion, but none came.

"Well, we will just need to work on that one, but I think for now, Franky needs to complete the first task," said Ethel. "If your guide told you to stay with your plan, then there is a reason."

"I'll go with you," said Shawn.

"I'll go too," said Benjamin.

"No, you need to keep the rest of them safe, take Ethel and Brandy home, and get their houses ready. I think it's best if it's just me and Shawn," Franky said.

"Okay," said Benjamin, "but don't you dare make a move to face them without me."

"Agreed," said Shawn.

Franky remained silent.

"Franky, give me your word," said Benjamin.

"I give you my word," he said at last.

Josette gave a small groan and grabbed her head.

"You all right, honey?" asked Ethel.

"Fine. There is not much they can give me that helps," said Josette. She turned to Franky. "You have to bring Phillip back to me, Franky," she said as she started to cry once more. "I'm pregnant."

The drive to Ruskin was quiet, as both Franky and Shawn were lost in their own thoughts. The revelation that Phillip was going to be a father filled Franky with both hope and dread. Now more than ever, he knew that news would make Phillip the happiest man in the world. Even though he had sworn off children, Franky knew deep down inside that Phillip Parker would make the world's greatest dad. After all, he had been his father figure for many years. *Let's just hope he gets the chance to raise his own child*, thought Franky to himself.

While Franky was thinking about Phillip's fate, Shawn was thinking about what they would say when they got there and how they could possibly find out from people who probably had no idea what their nephew was up to where Phillip and Mary were being held as hostages.

As they pulled into the parking lot, they saw that the place was open, but few cars were out front. It was still a half hour before noon, so they had beat the lunch crowd. "I think we should just go with us being college friends of Joe's. They must know he is studying abroad and would have no idea who any of his friends are," said Shawn.

"Fine," said Franky with no true conviction. His eyes showed that his mind was a million miles away.

Shawn grabbed Franky's face and turned it so that Franky was looking him straight in the eyes. "Look, Franky, you need to get your head in the game. I know a lot of shit is going on, but right now, I need you to have your shit together."

Franky's eyes seemed to clear, and he forced a smile. "You're right. Let's do this."

As Franky and Shawn walked into the restaurant, a pretty woman wearing a beautiful oriental-style dress greeted them.

"How many?" she asked as she approached.

"Well, actually, we are not here for lunch. We are looking for Joe Chung. He is our college buddy, and we thought he might be here. He talks about this place all the time," said Shawn.

"Oh, Joe. He is my nephew," she said. "Come in. I get you tea."

From inside the kitchen came the booming voice of a man speaking Chinese.

In return, the woman yelled back just as loudly. When she was done, she turned back to Franky and Shawn. "That my husband. He don't speak English well. Come. Have a seat," she said, pointing to a small table near the door. As they sat, she ran off and then quickly returned with two cups and a small craft of tea. "Joe not been here for two days. Don't know what he is up to, but it's nice to see he has friends all the way over in Ireland. I worry about him."

There was another loud exchange between the man in the kitchen and the woman. The only thing Franky and Shawn understood was the word *Joe*.

"Sorry. He a pain in my ass. Love him, but still a pain," she said with a smile.

"Man, we were so hoping to catch him. We are

going to Miami for a couple days and thought he might want to go."

That put an even bigger smile on the woman's face as she stood next to their table. "Oh, I wish I know how to get ahold of him. He checked out of his motel. I don't know where he is, but I am so grateful you think of him. I know he is around. He promised to stay until we open the new restaurant. My husband even offer him a job if he stay."

Franky and Shawn looked at each other. "He never said anything about a new restaurant. Where is it, if you don't mind me asking?" asked Franky a little too eagerly.

"Right down US 41. They are building big housing complex back on a new road. Hundreds of houses. We will be open just as they start selling. It all built. We just need to buy from kitchen supplier," she said with a sense of pride. "Then we have two locations."

"What is the name of the development?" asked Shawn. "It sounds exciting."

"Oh, what the name?" said the woman. Then she yelled into the kitchen so loudly that Franky had to cover his ears.

"Queen Palms!" the man yelled.

"That's right. Queen Palms," the woman said with a smile.

"Well, we don't want to take any more of your

time. Tell Joe we will get ahold of him later, okay?" said Franky, standing. "It was so nice to meet you."

"Yes, thank you so much for the tea," Shawn said.

"Oh no, thank you for being Joe's friends. He needs friends," she said, giving them a big smile.

With that, they walked out to the truck as fast as they could.

"I know what you are thinking," said Shawn, getting behind the wheel. "But remember what we told Benjamin."

"I know, I know, but we don't even know if they are there. Let's just drive by to see."

Even though Brandy knew she was returning to a mess, she was not prepared for what she saw. Her trailer was far worse than the hotel room. They had gone through all her drawers and the cabinets in her kitchen and thrown all her food from the refrigerator onto the floor. They had gone through all her important papers and scattered them everywhere, and her bedroom looked as if a bomb had gone off. Her bed was off the frame, with the box spring against one wall and the mattress against another. Benjamin started at once to get it back on the frame.

Ethel went over to check her trailer as Brandy assessed the damage to hers. Ethel's home was just as Tony had said: untouched. She made her way to the bathroom, and from the linen closet, she pulled out a shoebox. She tucked it under her arm and returned to Brandy's.

The cleanup work took the rest of the morning. Starting at the back of the double-wide, they made their way toward the front and only stopped once to eat a small lunch before starting again. Around one o'clock, they were finished except for the kitchen. Benjamin went out to the van and returned with salt, which he poured generously under each entrance to the trailer. He then walked over to Ethel's and repeated the steps.

While Benjamin was next door, Ethel took sage out of the shoebox and put it in a bowl. With it lit, she walked from room to room, demanding that any spirits in the house leave immediately. Once she had covered every inch of space, she walked out the door and back to her own house. Benjamin had just finished with the salt when she came through the door. He did not need to ask what she was up to; he knew. "How is Brandy holding up?" he asked, following Ethel down the hall to her back bedroom.

"Brandy is as strong as they come," said Ethel. "She'll be all right."

"You both are remarkable women," said Benjamin.

Ethel smiled. "Yes, I think we are too. We have

been through a lot, the two of us, and now that we are together again, it will take the devil himself to pull us apart."

Benjamin followed Ethel through the rest of the house as she did her clearing. She asked Benjamin about Ireland and told him she had always wanted to go there. He told her that when this was all over, Ethel and Brandy were welcome to stay at his house to take a long vacation. Ethel liked the thought of traveling again.

When they got back to Brandy's, Shawn and Franky were already there. Brandy was hurriedly fixing them both lunch.

"We found them," said Shawn.

Joe woke up to the sound of moans and the sun blaring in his eyes. His body was sore from sleeping on the floor, and his stomach rumbled from hunger. Looking around, he did not see Banthom or Mathew. Those two didn't seem to require sleep. From outside, he heard construction coming from across the street. Maybe he would sneak off and go to his aunt and uncle's for a quick bite, he thought.

Sitting up, he looked around at the new location they had built. It was a lot larger than the old restaurant. The place had only two rooms: the large kitchen in back and the dining area up front. The walls were all bare, and the kitchen was empty of equipment. Between the two rooms were two full-sized swinging doors. His aunt had insisted it be a sit-down restaurant from day one—no more buffet or open service window. Food would be brought from the kitchen, not passed through a hole in the wall. The place was going to have class. Though the place looked complete, his uncle had told him it needed to pass inspection before they could deliver any of the kitchen equipment or furniture. He remembered his uncle complaining about the wiring and how much the sprinkler system had cost. He'd talked about meeting wind codes for hurricanes and about the additional cost of flood insurance.

Once again, he heard loud moans coming from the new kitchen area. He tried to ignore the sound, but it seemed to be getting louder. *What the hell is going on in there?* he thought. Early that morning, they had returned with Mary and Phillip. When Joe had gone in to lie down, they'd been tied up and lying on the floor. How beautiful Mary had looked. He knew she hated him right now, but that would change. Even after everything that had happened, including all the fear and all the wicked deeds he was a part of, he knew she was worth it. Banthom had promised he could make her fall in love with him. He could not wait for her to finally be his and make love to him willingly. He wanted to feel her touch upon his skin.

This time, it was more than just a moan he heard; it was a scream of pain. He got up and hurried through the doors to the kitchen.

"The moment we saw Ethel's car there, we knew," said Franky before finishing the soup and sandwich Brandy had prepared.

"So what are we waiting for?" asked Ethel.

Benjamin smiled at her. "No. I'm sorry, but you two are staying put this time."

"God only knows what we are going to find when we get there," added Shawn, taking his plate to the kitchen. "We can't go with our original plan of salting the outside and burning the whole place down with them in it. Not until we get Phillip and Mary out of there."

"I'm not thinking past getting them both the hell out," said Franky. "That should be our only goal."

"We will have to take it as it comes. When we get there, we will need to assess the situation. With any luck, the bastards will be somewhere else."

"Look, I would feel better if we went back to the hospital and looked after Josette. I have a feeling she is not out of danger yet," Brandy told Ethel. "Maybe we can take some salt and, if need be, put a barrier between her and Gurney. Gany? Whatever that bastard's name is."

"Danior. Gunari Danior," said Franky. "It's important you remember it."

"Well, I, for one, think that is a great idea," said Benjamin in agreement.

"Can you leave us the truck?" asked Brandy. "Those bastards have my keys."

"And my car," said Ethel.

"Everything we need is in the van," said Benjamin. "I don't think we will need the truck."

"Fine by me," Franky said, reaching into his pocket and throwing the keys across the table.

"Well, I, for one, am tired of waiting. Let's go get this thing done," said Shawn. "No matter what happens, I cannot take the waiting any longer."

"I agree," said Benjamin. Without another word, the three men rose to their feet and headed toward the door. Franky turned and gave Brandy a big hug. Not saying another word, he turned and followed the other two men out the door.

"Well, what do you think their chances are?" Ethel asked Brandy.

"You don't want to know what I think," said Brandy.

"Dear, I think I already do, 'cause I'm thinking the same thing," Ethel replied.

As the three men traveled to their destination, the skies darkened and then suddenly opened up. Lightning strike after lightning strike lit up the sky. As they drove on through the rain, they talked about how to make their approach. They decided they would park a block up the road and make their way on foot. That way, if they needed to rearm themselves with flammables, the van would not be that far out of reach.

Once they found the perfect spot, they stopped, and before Shawn and Franky could even exit the van, Benjamin reached into the back and pulled out a leather case. He opened it, exposing three handguns. "These are fully loaded forty-four-caliber Magnum revolvers," said Benjamin. "They may not kill the bastards, but they sure as shit will slow them down."

"It will kill Joe," said Franky. "That's good enough for me."

Along with the handguns, each man strapped on a utility belt complete with a Zippo lighter, a can of WD-40, hair spray, holy water, a cross, salt, and a book of matches. Shawn, as always, insisted on bringing his small Canon camera, which was always hanging around his neck, while Franky insisted on carrying a small bucket of gasoline. After all, it had worked for him before.

The building was far back off US 41, so with any luck, no one from the road would see them sneaking into an empty building. Crouching down as far as they could, they stayed to the uncleared row of thick palmetto bushes and cabbage palms. There were two large windows in front, so they inched along the far right side, where there were no windows or doors. When they reached the front of the building, they made their way directly under the first window. There they were well protected from the rain by an awning running the entire length of the building. Franky held up a single finger and then inched upward so that he could peek inside. He did not even make it all the way to the window seal before he stopped. "Water by the road," he whispered, setting down his bucket. He then went back the same way they had just come.

"What the hell?" whispered Benjamin.

Shawn shrugged as he watched Franky disappear into the hedgerow. "Maybe he left something in the van."

Within a few minutes, Franky was back. Both men gave him questioning looks. "I'll tell you later," he said.

This time, Benjamin held up a single finger as he slowly stood and took a fast peek into the first room. It was empty. He shook his head so the other two knew that Phillip and Mary were not there. Then he pointed to the right side of the building. They moved quickly but quietly to the back. There was a door, but there were no windows to peek through.

"Do we go for it?" asked Shawn softly.

Benjamin and Franky both nodded in agreement. With that, Shawn reached up and tried the back door. It was unlocked. Slowly, he opened it, making sure not to make a sound. From his location, that room too looked empty. He gave a wave of his hand and started to walk inside. There on the far wall, Shawn saw Phillip and Mary, and he had to suppress a gasp. Franky, hearing his reaction, pushed his way in to see. Once Franky saw them, he threw all caution to the wind and rushed headlong into the room.

Phillip and Mary were standing next to each other in handcuffs secured above their heads by hooks drilled deep into a thick piece of two-by-four. Their naked bodies were stained red, with blood oozing from large scratch marks across their chests, just below their necks. Neither one made any indication he or she was even alive.

Franky put his bucket on the floor, rushed to Phillip, and grabbed his arm. "He has a pulse," he said. Then he put his ear to his chest. "And I can hear him breathing."

Phillip let out a slight moan, reaffirming Franky's findings.

Shawn instinctually started to snap pictures one after another.

Franky looked over at Mary and saw Benjamin with one hand on Mary's wrist and the other on her chest. He looked over at Franky, his eyes filling with tears, and shook his head.

"Look at their feet," said Shawn, still snapping photos. On the floor just in front of them was a circle etched into the floor. In the middle was a pentagram with peculiar markings, and scattered on the floor was what appeared to be broken pottery—brown bowls covered with strange writing written in blood. Right in the middle of the circle was the grimoire. Shawn started to reach for it but stopped short.

Suddenly, the back door slammed shut. It was Banthom. He had been standing behind it all that time. On the floor at his feet lay the half-eaten body of Joe. Shawn reached for his gun but never even got close. With a wave of Banthom's hand, all three men went slamming into the wall, where they remained a good two feet off the floor. Their abilities to move and speak were gone. They all tried to reach for their weapons, but it was useless.

"Mathew, will you kindly relieve these gentlemen of their little toys?" Banthom asked as he moved his hand once more, and they all came crashing to the floor.

Through the swinging double doors between the dining room and kitchen walked Mathew. He had a large grin on his face and a gun in his hand. He grabbed Benjamin, who was still unable to move an inch in retaliation; lifted him to his feet; and then slammed him face-first against the wall, where he proceeded to pat him down. He removed his belt, his gun, and everything else he had brought with him and threw them onto the floor. When he was satisfied, Mathew moved on to Shawn and then Franky.

"Now, let's get these gentlemen into the other room, shall we?" said Banthom.

Mathew did as instructed; he grabbed Benjamin and Shawn by their collars and dragged them into the dining room, where he dropped them roughly onto the floor. Their limp bodies hit with a loud thud. Next came Franky, whom Mathew halfway flung through the doors, causing him to land directly on Shawn.

Looking up at Banthom as he ceremoniously emerged from the kitchen, Franky noticed for the first time that he was whole. Banthom sauntered across the room, stopped on the other side in front of the big windows, and then turned to the three men on the floor. He gave a nod to Mathew, who joined him, still holding the gun and pointing it directly at them.

"I am going to release you, but one wrong move, and I will kill you. You do not want to end up like your friend Joe, do you? Funny thing. It seems he didn't like the way I was treating the girl Mary. You see, the fool honestly thought I was going to give her to him. I do not do well with people disagreeing will me. I was so hoping my last meal would have been that sweet little medium of yours, as I would have liked to have a bit of her power, but the last turned out to be that pathetic creature instead."

With that, Banthom waved his hand once more, and the group on the floor started to feel the luxury of movement once more.

"Your friend Joe was a clever one—I will give him that," Banthom said, looking up at the sprinklers evenly placed along the celling. "Even if you had used your little flame makers, he said these things would put out the fire in seconds. I think I like these modern times." He turned and again faced the men on the floor. "Here are your choices: you can join me and be a part of my new cult, or you can die."

Based solely on his appearance, it was hard to believe the man was in any way evil. He almost looked majestic. He had a handsome young face; long, flowing brown hair; and bright, beautiful brown eyes. *How can someone who looks so regal be such a monster?* thought Franky.

"You rot in hell," said Benjamin.

"Benjamin, don't be such a bore" said Banthom.

"Let me kill this one," Mathew said.

"Patience, my friend," Banthom said to Mathew.

"All in good time." Turning his attention to Shawn, Banthom continued. "Shawn, a good-looking young man like you could bring many potential females—and males, for that matter—to me, and I could make them new members of my family."

"Never!" exclaimed Shawn. Before he could say more, his sweet Samantha appeared, kneeling at Banthom's feet. Her complexion was gray, her hair was matted, and her eyes were sunken into her skull, but he could tell it was her.

"Well, let's not be too hasty," Banthom said, holding the helpless Samantha by her hair. "You see, her spirit belongs to me now. Your sweet Sam—what a shame."

"No!" screamed Shawn.

It was obvious to Franky that Shawn was seeing something, but he didn't know what. To him, Banthom and Mathew stood alone on the other side of the room.

"I could make her do such dirty little things," Banthom said, reaching down to stroke her breast. "Or maybe I could just torture the bitch for eternity." With that, he reached down and, with the middle finger of each hand, reached into her open mouth. He hooked his fingers onto her cheeks and started to pull his hands apart. Her mouth stretched as far as humanly possible.

"What about now, my friend?" he asked with a malevolent grin.

"No!" Shawn yelled.

"It's up to you, Shawn. Join me, and I will let her pass on; if not, I will tear her soul apart." With that, he applied more pressure, and Sam's lips began to tear just below the nose and above her chin. Shawn watched as she struggled in pain.

"What about now?" said Banthom, his grin growing larger.

"My God, stop!" yelled Shawn once more.

Banthom pulled again, this time ripping half the girl's face apart.

Shawn hollered in pain.

"It isn't real, Shawn," said Franky. "Close your eyes. He is a deceiver. It's not real."

Shawn closed his eyes and hung his head. "No, no, no, no," he said repeatedly.

Just then, a loud bang came from the kitchen. They heard wood groan and then splinter. An unnatural scream of agony echoed through the air. It was Phillip. Franky knew it was Phillip, and he was in pain.

Banthom looked up. "Well, it starts," he said. "Finally, I will see my family's quest complete." Franky's mind raced. He tried to think of everything Josette had said, including all the instructions she had given him and every word Kip had told her. Then, with a look of determination in his eyes, he said directly to Banthom, "Tell me—how is that Gypsy slut mother of yours, Gunari?"

All of Banthom's attention swung straight to Franky. "What did you just say to me?"

"We know all about you, Gunari Danior— bastard son of a Gypsy witch whore!" yelled Franky.

Banthom reached out an arm with his hand open wide. Franky felt the grip of Banthom's hand on his throat even though he was nowhere near him. He felt him pulling his body toward him, and his toes barely touched the floor as he made his way across the room. When he was close enough, Banthom grabbed him by the throat and held him at arm's length. "Now you die, Mr. Lake."

The gunshot blast that followed tore through the air. Franky saw half of Banthom's head simply blown away. He could feel the monster's blood splashing across his face. Time seemed to stand still. Mathew stood staring at his master in shock. When reality finally seemed to hit him, he made a mad dash to help, but then came the second shot, which went right through the back of Mathew's skull. For a brief second, Banthom's grip tightened, and then he fell to the floor at Franky's feet. That was when Franky saw Brandy. She was outside the front window, holding a smoking shotgun.

Shawn, full of fear and rage, stood and immediately ran into the kitchen. At once, he grabbed the pail of gasoline and pulled a Zippo from one of the utility belts. That was when he noticed they were gone—Mary and Phillip were no longer hanging from the wall. Where Phillip once had been bound, the board was broken in half, and below, his handcuffs lay in tiny pieces upon the floor. Looking up once more, he noticed that Mary's cuffs still hung from their hook. They were not unlocked or broken, but she was not there. Shawn reached for his camera, snapped off a couple shots, and then looked down and saw the grimoire lying in the same spot as before. He took one more shot of the floor, grabbed the book, picked up the bucket, and headed back into the other room. As soon as he cleared the doorway, he tossed the book underhanded across the room. "Catch!" he yelled to Franky as he continued running toward Banthom. He splashed half the contents of the bucket onto Banthom and half onto Mathew. His only hope was that the rain had not diluted the gasoline too much.

Franky took a single step back and caught the book with one hand, but that one step was not far enough. Banthom, with blood gushing from where the left side of his face once had been, reached up once more and grabbed him by the ankle. He gave a hard jerk, and Franky went face-first onto the floor.

Benjamin ran across the room and started kicking Banthom with everything he had, trying to get him to release his grip on Franky. Shawn, on the other hand, had a different solution. He lit the Zippo and let it fly, hitting Banthom squarely on the back. A small flame started climbing up his back toward his hair. Banthom, releasing Franky, jumped to his feet and looked up at the silent sprinklers.

Franky too jumped to his feet. "They don't work when you shut off the fucking water, asshole," he said while giving Banthom a good kick in the middle of his gut. The blow sent him flying backward, and he landed next to Mathew. Mathew too started to burn.

"Pray, Benjamin. For God's sake, say the prayer!" yelled Franky.

Without hesitation, Benjamin dropped to one knee and started to recite the Lord's Prayer in Latin.

Mathew's body at once burst into flames with a loud whooshing sound. Banthom stood once more, fully engulfed in flames, and made a mad dash for the door, but when he hit the door, it did not give; it was as if it had been constructed of solid stone. The impact sent Banthom to the floor one more time.

As Benjamin continued to pray, Franky could not believe what he was seeing with his own eyes. All the spirits killed by Banthom's evil deeds came forward. Half in shock and half in fear, he watched them come from all corners of the room. Some gray and battered and some blue and stinking of the sea, they all appeared. The last to enter were a little girl and her brother; Franky knew she must have been the one from Banthom House—his first kill.

All at once, Banthom's body exploded into thousands of small pieces, leaving only a shining specter floating in the middle of the room. From the specter came small balls of light, each traveling to a specific spirit in the room. Once the orbs of light reached their destinations, the spirits simply disappeared. When light reached the small girl, she and her brother turned to Franky—they were beautiful, healthy-looking children once more—and smiled at him in thanks. Then, in an instant, they vanished.

Suddenly, they all felt the room begin to shake. Smoke was rising from the floor. "We need to get Phillip and Mary and get the hell out of here!" yelled Franky.

"They are not there," replied Shawn, but Franky either didn't hear or didn't care. He started toward the kitchen.

Just then, the front door swung open with a load bang. "Get the hell out of there!" Ethel's voice said from outside.

Shawn roughly grabbed Franky by the waist and pulled him backward out the front door, where he stumbled backward and then fell onto the hard pavement.

Benjamin finished the prayer with an "Amen" and then rushed out just in time. He managed to get a good ten feet away from the building before an explosion knocked him to the ground next to Franky.

"Look!" yelled Ethel, pointing upward.

The top of the building was all but gone, and in the middle of the rubble, they all saw a large red claw protruding from far below the earth. Long black nails reached toward the dark sky. Just above them, the tiny specter that once had been Banthom hovered motionlessly. In a flash, the claw snatched the specter out of the air, and a loud scream blasted forth, followed by a bolt of lightning and a loud clap of thunder. Then, as quickly as the claw had appeared, it was gone, sucked back into the ground from which it had come.

"The devil claims his own," said Ethel.

Franky stood in the still-pouring rain and looked at Shawn. "Why? We could have saved them," he said.

"I'm sorry, Franky, but when I went in to get the bucket, they were not there," replied Shawn.

Franky ran toward Shawn and pushed him hard to the ground. "You're lying! You let them both die."

"You don't know that," said Benjamin, grabbing hold of Franky from behind.

"I'm not lying. I tell you they were gone," Shawn

said. "I have proof." He pointed to his camera. "I got the shots."

"Look, we need to get the hell out of here before the cops come," said Brandy.

"She's right," said Benjamin.

Shawn stood, walked over to Franky, and gave him a hug. "I know it's hard to believe right now, but I would never lie to you."

Franky, reluctant at first, hugged him back. "I know," he said, sobbing openly into Shawn's shoulder. "I know."

It was hard to believe a week had passed since their duel with death at the hands of a powerful witch. Every attempt to locate Mary and Phillip had failed; still, Franky was not willing to give up. As he sat at the kitchen table at Brandy's, he watched the old woman make a hot pastrami on rye at the stove. How incredible she and Ethel had been. Franky knew now that Brandy never had had any intention of going to see Josette; that excuse had been her way of getting the keys to the truck without prolonging the argument.

If they had not arrived when they had, he and all the rest most likely would have been dead. *Thank God she's a good shot*, thought Franky with a smile. It was Ethel, though, who had laid the salt line in front of the door. If not, the beast might have made it outside and had his flames extinguished by the rain.

Franky smiled while thinking about when Ethel had pulled out her spare keys as they'd gotten ready to leave. "At least they didn't hurt my baby," she had said. With all that had happened, she had been worried about getting her car scratched. Yes, they were two crazy old women—that was for sure—but those two amazing women were also his guardian angels.

"You want mustard or mayo?" asked Brandy from the kitchen. "I have hot mustard if you want that."

"That sounds great," Franky replied.

Benjamin had been the first to leave. His reasons for taking off the next morning were clear. First, he needed to take the evil book away and put it wherever he'd put the first one. "Somewhere it can never be used again," he had told them, not divulging to anyone where that was.

His second priority, of course, was the death of Tony, his employee, who had been found outside the hotel where Benjamin had booked three suites. He was not afraid of going to jail—they had nothing on him, and he knew that—but he knew the cops would talk to the same employees Benjamin and his group had talked out of calling the police. He knew he would at the very least be detained. That he did not want. Thank God he was the only one who had put his name on any of the bills. Before he'd left, he'd handed Brandy a credit card. "There is a hundred-grand limit on this thing. Everyone else will need to go home eventually, so I am counting on you to hire the best damn private investigator you can to help track down Mary and Phillip," he'd said.

The next morning, Brandy had hired a Tampa firm to take the case. She'd also put in a missing person's report with the local police department.

As for Josette, she'd come home from the hospital the day after Benjamin left. Franky remembered how hard it had been that first night to tell her that the father of her unborn child was gone and maybe dead.

"He is not dead," Josette had replied with a smile.

"Have you spoken to Kip again?" he had asked.

"No, I just feel it. He is not dead," she'd said with such confidence that Franky felt a huge weight had been lifted off his shoulders.

Josette had left for England two days after Benjamin. She needed to go home to rest and take a break from everyone and everything. She had promised that when she got her head around everything that had taken place and her body had healed, she would leave for Dublin. There, with Benjamin's help, she would search Banthom House for the hidden scroll that Kip had requested she find. She seemed convinced that somehow the parchment would help them find Phillip and Mary. If she found it and it was of use, she would return to the States to help in the pursuit. However, for now, she needed to go home.

Shawn had been the last to leave. He'd agreed he would return in a heartbeat if there was even a clue to Mary and Phillip's whereabouts. In the meantime, he was going to try to patch things up with his parents. He had confided in Franky that he thought it was highly unlikely any of his efforts would make a difference, but still, he wanted to give it one more try. After that, he was planning on leaving California for good. He needed a change, a way to move forward with his life. He knew he could never run away from the pain of losing Sam, but he could allow himself some happiness. Before he'd left, he'd given Franky copies of all the photos from inside the restaurant. There it was, as clear as day: Phillip and Mary had in fact been gone when the building burned. For days, Franky had spent hours upon hours flipping through the photos, studying each one over and over again.

As for Franky, he'd called the University of Michigan and declined their offer. When the summer was over, if he had made no progress in finding Mary and Phillip, he would return to Michigan, back to living in Phillip's house, and teach next year at Parksville University. No matter what happened, he would never give up the search for Phillip. He had lost his mother, and he would not lose Phillip as well.

Brandy walked over to the kitchen table and set a plate in front of Franky: a large, heaping sandwich cut in half and pulled apart with a pile of potato chips in the middle. "You want some soup to go with this sandwich?" asked Brandy.

"No, I think I'm good," Franky said.

AFTERWORD

As Franky ate his sandwich, Benjamin crossed the square with the book tucked under his right arm. Though the night was cool for that time of year, Benjamin was ringing wet with sweat. As he passed the Egyptian obelisk, he felt overwhelmed. The semicircular colonnades, with their massive columns, always seemed to remind him of how small a single person was in the grand scheme of things.

A few tourists still lingered around, but Benjamin did not take any notice of them as he walked on. He could feel all the statues of popes and martyrs atop the colonnades watching his progress. When he finally made his way to the front of the basilica, a single figure dressed in a white cassock came out to meet him. On his head, the man wore a small white skullcap. His kind, round face held a large smile.

Benjamin knelt before him. The man walked up to him, and Benjamin reached out, took the man's hand, and kissed a gold crucifix shaped into a ring. Gently, the man reached down and put his hand on Benjamin's chin. "Rise, my son," he said softly.

Benjamin rose and handed him the book without saying a word.

"You have done well," said the man with a big smile. "Your family's oath to the church has been fulfilled." Then, to Benjamin's surprise, the man reached down, grabbed Benjamin's hand, and looked at the ring upon his finger. "And Father Marcus may now rest in peace." Then, looking Benjamin straight in the eyes, he whispered, "You wear this well." With that, the man turned and headed back into the basilica.

Benjamin simply turned and walked away.

About the Author

Rodney Wetzel graduated with honors from Western Michigan University and continued his education at Spring Arbor College. When not writing horror, he spends his time working as a grant writer and Senior Planner. He is the author of Fritz. He and his wife live outside Tampa, Florida, where he is currently at work on his third book.

Printed in the United States
By Bookmasters